Predilection

Mary Parker

PublishAmerica
Baltimore

ISBN: 978-1-60749-271-9 (softcover)
ISBN: 978-1-4489-1747-1 (hardcover)
PUBLISHED BY PUBLISHAMERICA, LLLP
www.publishamerica.com
Baltimore

Printed in the United States of America

To my parents, for everything.

Table of Contents

Orchestra of Echoes

Everything was darkness: an endless, all-consuming black. The woman was sure she was awake; her thoughts were not clouded, she was simply opening her eyes to oblivion. She could hear the soft clicking of her eyelids as she blinked, but nothing appeared except the wide darkness that threatened to swallow her. She felt incredibly weak, her legs and arms aching and heavy, but she could move and speak, although her voice was hoarse and she could not bear to hear it. She was kneeling on the ground, as if praying for salvation to the black magnitude. She felt around her and realized she was surrounded by earth that was gritty but slick, like dirt turning into the beginnings of mud.

The woman rose to her feet and took a hesitant step forward. She put her hands to her sides to balance herself and knew she was walking through an earthen tunnel, an endless hallway.

Suddenly, out of the heavy silence came a tight tapping sound, rhythmical and precise. She followed the sound, hands outstretched and searching like a blind woman. She was lightheaded and felt off-balance, but her legs moved with determination as if possessed by something else altogether. The earth around her, the solidity in the dark, was remarkably even. She felt no fear of tripping. It seemed to the woman that as she walked the tapping grew louder but also seemed farther away. It

9

echoed and reverberated, enveloping her. She felt like her eyes were rattling in her skull.

The woman's fingertips felt bruised; her feeling in them was lessening, but she knew that the earth around her had grown damper. Her footsteps sank with each step, hard to pull up and releasing with a sickening, fleshy *pop*. She wanted to turn back but could not. Her body would not allow it. She was being tugged from her hips, forcibly pulled in half. Soon she noticed that everything around her was not just wet, but sticky. A metallic taste began in the back of her throat, and coupled with the unmistakable smell invading her nostrils: blood.

Maybe, the woman thought, I am not underground at all. Maybe the darkness surrounding me, the humidity pressing down, is not that at all, but blood, a tunnel of blood swirling around me, sucking me in. The tapping continued to grow louder, bouncing off the blood-walls, pounding into her temples. She became very tired.

The ground dropped from beneath her.

She fell face-first into the coppery mud, finding it full of small, hard chunks, like gravel—or bone. The blood-earth covered her, weighing down her clothes, matting her hair to her face; pieces of gravel-bone embedded themselves into her sore skin, burrowing down.

The tapping suddenly stopped, leaving a newfound silence more terrifying than anything she had ever known. In the silence she was left with nothing but herself and it was terrible. Her brain tried to seize some sensation from the air; it needed to move, to roam about the darkness, find its hidden secrets. But it found only empty air, and was forced to search within itself for sustenance. It drug up memories the woman wished with her entire being to forget; it brought sights before her retinas that brought tears, put feelings in her chest that made her breathing labored.

Just as abruptly as it had stopped, the tapping resumed, even louder than before, showing the expanse of the place she was now in. She knew the source of the tapping was near. She felt herself, without thinking about it, get up and walk. She did not need to steady herself on the walls now. Her mind was blank except for one purpose: just keeping walking. Her eyes closed and she took in the dormant rapture. In a gracious reprieve her mind had stopped. She was outside herself, outside all consciousness. The darkness that had engulfed her just moments earlier had found its way inside her and she became the darkness. Just. Keep. Walking.

The tapping became a steady drumming, fluid and beckoning.

"Open your eyes," said a deep voice that pierced through the darkness. "Look at me and *see.*"

Her lips quivered and her chest trembled. She knew this voice. It was from her past somewhere, yet distinctly familiar as if it had been born inside her.

"Open your eyes," It said again. "Open them *now.*"

Its tone was sharp; upon its piercing command, the woman did as she was told.

She had known the voice as soon as she heard it, but when she looked she was certain that she did not know this…*thing.* It looked at her with gaping, deep, black, soulless eyes. Its entire body was long and slender, and a foggy, reflective color, as if covered in slime. The fingers that had been tapping were long with knobby knuckles and thin, arching fingernails that were at least four inches long, jagged, and pointed. The Thing had no face, just black, cavernous eyes, sharp fingernails like weapons, and gnashing teeth that made a sound like weeping. When she looked at It she felt she did not know It, but did, in some deep corner of her mind.

The Thing smiled at her, a malicious, stretched grin, and snapped its teeth together, snarling, like some dog-threat, and to ignore the horror of its mouth she looked into its eyes. In them she saw an orchestra of echoes: all the pain and fatigue of her life reflected in a sublime pleasure, a flowing crescendo. In it sounded everything she thought she believed, everything she wanted but would not acknowledge, all her remorse and hatred, her sin and sickness; all her lust and errors, her hypocritical purposes, her lies; her death; her suffering and self-destruction, her self-imposed agony.

She saw and knew herself. She was appalled but could not refuse.

"You *belong* here," It said.

She did not refute, but walked toward It, arms extended, reaching for its sweet solace.

1

No one realized what was happening. No one noticed that the darkness of their nights was lasting a little longer. They didn't see the shadows in their windows. It seemed they just assumed that the sky was perpetually cloudy, as of late—they didn't recognize that the sun itself was darkening.

They had no idea.

* * *

After the first nightmare, the boy believed he had not seen the monster at all. His parents were right: there was no monster in his bedroom doorway. He had no reason not to accept what his parents had told him—the next night the monster did not return, and the boy slept easily because he thought the horror had passed. But after a few more sleepless nights he began to think otherwise.

In his nightmares, the figure always showed up after the flood began in his room, stepping into view once the water had surrounded him, begun to seep into his bedclothes, and started to turn red. Later when he woke up, the monster was standing in his doorway, its head bowed. He was sure of it. But he figured he would wait to tell his parents again. His mother was very tired and his father busy. He should wait a few more nights and see if the monster would go away. He tried to convince himself that his parents were right: they had to be. Just one more night, he told himself, every night.

Later, in the darkness, when the figure looked up and smiled at him, his scream told his parents more than words could ever say.

* * *

Caleb Sampson had been in the Minaret Children's Institute (a subsidiary of the Minaret Home for the Mentally Disabled) for eight days when he disappeared. During her night rounds, Nurse Melanie noticed that the door to Caleb's room was open. *That's strange*, she thought, *he should have closed it by now.* At least four times a night Caleb's door would have to be opened by one of the night nurses. The "sleep-time rules," as they were called in the pediatric wing, were simple: no talking after lights out, ring for a nurse before you leave your room, although the only place you could go at night was to the bathroom, and keep your door open at all times.

Caleb incessantly refused to keep his door open. Even though he had experienced only one night terror during his stay, the monster, he said, would come in if his door was open. One night he had even broken apart the small plastic chair each child had in their room and jammed the pieces around the knob, stuffed them between the door and the jamb so it couldn't be opened. The next morning everything except the bed, his clothes, and a few select toys were removed from his room.

His doctor announced to him that the monster could not enter the hospital, the security guards wouldn't let it; he was safe, door closed or not. Caleb threw himself into a rage. It took three nurses to restrain him enough for a sedative to be administered. It was the first time the child had shown aggression toward anyone in the hospital, and his parents assured the doctor that there was no past history of violence. So the doctor came up with a plan: let him close his door, but once he's had time to fall asleep, open it again. He expected Caleb would grow tired of repeatedly having to get up and close the door and would eventually stop getting up at night altogether. But Caleb maintained that his door had to be shut or the nightmares would continue.

When she saw the door was still open, Nurse Melanie was relieved that Caleb had not closed it, but still cautious. She hoped Dr. Pitchell's plan had worked, and that the boy was making progress, or was at least deeply asleep. Usually, Caleb's room was the first visited in Hall 3B (the Jet Plane Hallway, as the children called it, named for the pictures of airplanes painted in "cheerful" colors on the walls) but since his door was still open Melanie decided to check the other children's rooms first. She didn't want to take the chance of disturbing him before she had to. But when she saw the thin trail of blood coming from Caleb's doorway into the hall, her breath caught in her throat.

She looked inside the room; the covers on the bed were pulled back messily, his pillow thrown in a corner. The trail started by the bed and stopped no more than a foot out of the door. *Maybe he just had a bloody nose*, Melanie thought. He had been getting those quite a bit lately. The first two nights Caleb stayed at Minaret he had woken up with nosebleeds in the early morning. Stress from adjusting to his new environment coupled with the stress of his night terrors, Dr. Pitchell said. *That's it*, Melanie told herself, *he had a bloody nose and ran to the bathroom without ringing us. I'll have to remind him to ring us no matter what*. But Caleb was not in the bathroom. She ran back to his room, looking in every corner, thinking she had not passed him in the hall, but he wasn't in there. She looked in all the rooms. He was not there either. She hurried to the nurse's station. None of the other nurses had seen him. The alarm was sounded.

Some of the tiny lights lining the top of the hallway began to spiral, the pink lights, which signaled a child was missing. They had put up the lights so that the children would not be disturbed by any loud alarms. Usually, the lights worked fine, but maintenance had to be called the next morning because the bulbs needed to be replaced. The night Caleb disappeared, whenever an adult passed under one of the pink lights, they turned blood red and would pop off until the adult was gone.

* * *

Caleb Sampson's file was removed from the Minaret archives and destroyed eight years after he disappeared, as were all of the children's files once they were gone from Minaret without readmission and/or reached the edge of eighteen. During the investigation that followed his disappearance, the police had turned up nothing, and the boy was assumed dead. Security cameras showed nothing. No one entered or left the hospital after seven that evening and no one had entered until three the next morning when the police finally arrived. All security were interviewed and given a polygraph, with no results. He simply vanished. Neglect charges were filed against Minaret and the local police force by Caleb's parents, but were later dropped because of insufficient funds. Soon Caleb was all but forgotten, just a sad memory in the long history of Minaret.

2

Hailey still refused to talk. She had been at Minaret for over a month, and no one had heard a sound escape her lips. She seemed a pleasant enough little girl: she was never violent with the other children or staff, she actively played with the toys presented to her, and always followed the rules. She was extremely intelligent as well, performing at one level above her age. Giving her the tests was a bit harder than with other children, since she wouldn't answer directly. She either pointed to the answer or wrote it down. She was hardly ever wrong.

She simply refused to speak.

After a week of silence, Dr. Pitchell asked her father if she was mute. He laughed and said no, bewildered by the question. Had she stopped talking at home?

Hailey's father looked at the floor, almost ashamed, and said, "It's been a while since I've heard her talk—all she'd done before I brought her here was scream."

But what the girl lacked in verbal skills she more than made up for in artistic abilities. She excelled during art time, which was really art therapy, and a very useful tool in evaluating the children of the Disturbed ward. Art therapy was used in conjunction with group play and individual one-on-one therapy. Its purpose was to evaluate the children's drawings, since they can be segmented into specific stages. Through these stages doctors could distinguish when a child is behind his age level, or in rare cases such as with certain types of autism, significantly ahead. It could also allow a child a medium to express their inner turmoil, such as low self-esteem (the child draws himself in a very scribbled, restricted manner while those around him are well-defined), feelings of powerlessness (arms and legs either absent or drawn too small and shriveled to be of any use), and depression (a child may use only one type of writing instrument and exert little investment in the picture).

Children's art skills are generally divided into four stages: the scribble stage, typically how a toddler colors and draws; the "pre-schematic" stage, between four and seven years, where children draw objects in a simple, symbolic fashion; the "schematic" stage, between seven and nine, when pictures take on more detail and depth of field; and finally the realism stage, around age ten, where images become standardized and attention to detail about how things look in real life is emphasized.

Hailey, at age six, was showing signs of all the stages in her drawings. When asked to draw her family, their bodies were more like stick figures, typical of the pre-schematic stage, but the actual figures were drawn in a scribbled fashion, with little attention to detail. When asked to draw her house, it was very ornate and more true-to-life. She also drew the landscape around the house, using depth of field to show hills and flowers that were far away. It was quite unusual. Since her behavior outside of the art therapy sessions was improving, she had begun to interact with more of the other children, shared her toys, and began to play—though still without speech—it was assumed her ability to express herself graphically provided an opening to release her frustrations.

One day, Hailey picked up a piece of paper and began to draw furiously. One of the nurses saw her, and walked over to observe. When she finished, Hailey turned to the nurse.

Without prompting she said, "This is the monster standing behind you. He is smiling because he is going to eat you." Her voice was raspy from lack of use, but firm.

The nurse immediately took the drawing, complimenting Hailey on how good it was, and brought it directly to Dr. Pitchell.

* * *

He was much older now than he had been when Caleb Sampson had stayed at Minaret, but his eye was still sharp, though the hair at his temples had grayed (it was the only hair he had left). Once he saw the drawing he knew he would not be able to forget the image of that monster or the frightened whispers that followed it, both from his staff and Hailey. He decided to call her father. They met twice weekly but this could not wait; he needed to know.

"Mr. Fischer? This is Dr. Pitchell."

"Is there something wrong?" Cael Fischer was always quick when it came to Hailey. There was no doubt he loved her very much and only wanted her to get better. What exactly needed to be remedied Dr. Pitchell still wasn't sure, but there was definitely a problem here.

"There's no need to worry, Mr. Fischer, she's fine, but I think you need to come in today, if you can. We need to talk about an issue that has come up with Hailey."

"An issue?"

"Yes... Cael, she's begun talking."

"What—just today? What did she say? Can I talk to her now?"

"I think it would be better if this was discussed in person. Can you come in this afternoon?"

"Of course; I'll need about an hour to cancel the meetings I had today but I'll make it half an hour."

* * *

Traffic was unusually congested for early afternoon, which was, of course, Cael Fischer's luck. Any time he needed to be somewhere, any time he had to get somewhere *urgently*, the world around him crawled to a stop. But crawling along, stop and go, he eventually got to the hospital. Finding a parking spot was a whole other issue, but eventually he found one of those too and sprinted to the elevator. As it lurched to the fifth floor he tried to calm himself down. He couldn't be upset in front of Hailey; that wouldn't fix anything. She didn't need any more to be upset about.

Ever since her mother had passed away, suddenly, from breast cancer six months before, Hailey had slowly withdrawn from the people around her—teachers, classmates and friends, and finally her father. One night she woke up screaming, shaking almost like she was having a seizure. It happened again the next night and the next.

"Night terrors," her pediatrician told him, "very common. Just try and soothe her as best you can. They'll stop on their own."

After four months the night terrors had not stopped, so Hailey stopped sleeping altogether, refused to eat, and then stopped talking. That was when the pediatrician recommended they pay a visit to Dr. Pitchell at Minaret.

"Isn't that a sanitarium?" Cael had asked.

"Yes," the doctor had said with no emotion. "Your daughter needs professional mental health care. Dr. Pitchell is a good man, I've known him for years; he'll take good care of her." He gave Cael the insurance referral and that was that.

In the month Hailey had been at Minaret he'd only seen her twice. She hadn't cried when he first left her; she just stood there staring at him blankly. The next time he came he hugged her but that was all. The last time he visited, a week ago, she showed him her favorite doll and flipped through a book while she sat on his lap, but it still seemed as if something was gone from her. She was just a silent, empty shell where a vibrant, sweet girl had once been. It tore him apart.

When he finally got to the Disturbed wing he was greeted by three lovely nurses behind a big desk which was covered by glass and flanked by two large guards.

"I need to see your ID," the heavyset guard said flatly. Once they typed God knows what into the computer—four times— and looked through their files, they called someone on their magical telephone and a man appeared near the door; they finally buzzed him through. This new guard was very nice, however. He had taken Cael to Hailey's wing both times he'd visited and was always pleasant enough. They wound through several hallways, past beige halls into ones with flowers and trains and happy faces painted on the walls. Dr. Pitchell was waiting for him, smiling. His eyes gave his concern away.

"Doctor, how is she?" Cael asked quickly. He had wanted not to seem too eager, but Dr. Pitchell's phone call had frightened him. The doctor sighed.

"Well, she's begun talking, but what she has to say is not very pleasant."

"What do you mean?"

"Let's get into my office and we can discuss it further, shall we?" They walked together to the far end of the play area. There were children coloring at plastic tables, little girls cooking pretend food at a kitchen set, boys pushing trucks around, *vroom-vrooming* to themselves. Cael was saddened because it was evident none of them were enjoying it. They went into Dr. Pitchell's office. His door was painted bright orange.

The inside of his office was cheery, a paler orange. His bookshelves and desk were nicely lacquered dark oak. There were diplomas on the wall and an overstuffed child-sized armchair in the corner, the edges of the armrests worn from many hours of little hands rubbing them. Dr. Pitchell took his seat behind the desk; Cael sat in the plain chair in front of it.

"Today," Dr. Pitchell started, "Hailey stopped playing dolls with some of the other girls and began to draw feverishly. One of the nurses saw her and watched her, thinking Hailey didn't notice, but when she was finished drawing Hailey showed the nurse her picture."

"—What's so strange about that?" Cael interrupted.

The doctor sighed again. He opened the file lying in front of him and pulled out a piece of paper. It had thick black lines all over it. He turned it so Cael could see. It was a picture of a monster, some strange creature, crudely drawn but plain enough. It had a very round head, solid black eyes, and large fangs. Cael was confused for a moment. Surely his daughter hadn't drawn that. Hailey's drawings from art therapy were not the nicest, sure; whenever she drew herself the picture was not of a happy girl, but they were never anything like this. Cael was going to say something else, but as soon as the thought formulated he forgot what he was going to ask. Or at least thought he had forgotten. Dr. Pitchell continued.

"When Hailey showed the nurse the drawing she told her this monster 'was smiling because it was going to eat' the nurse. Those were her first words." He let it sink in.

"What does this mean?" Cael asked. "What are we supposed to do?"

"There's no clear answer," Dr. Pitchell replied, "but one

thing's for sure: Hailey is much worse than we initially thought. There are definitely deep-rooted issues here. She hasn't shown any violence yet, but I'm afraid she might." He stopped, waiting for Cael to respond, but got nothing.

"When I asked her about this picture, she told me that this monster comes into her room every night and stares at her. She said it sometimes watches her play." He went silent for a moment.

"Cael, she said this monster has been coming to her room ever since her mother passed away. She says it looks at her like it's very hungry."

"Do you think Brenda's death hurt her that much?" Cael asked. Dr. Pitchell was glad to see he seemed genuinely concerned.

"I'm sorry, but I have to ask this," he said.

"Ask what?"

"Are *you* this monster?"

Silence.

"What the hell does that mean?" Cael stammered. "Why? I wouldn't, why would I, why…why would I come into her room?" His voiced trailed off.

"I understand losing a spouse is hard, and a man has urges, but—"

"You son of a bitch!" Cael stood up and drew his hand back, ready to strike.

"Mr. Fischer—"

"How dare you accuse me of such a thing? I would *never…*" he couldn't finish. He was so angry or sad—probably both—that he couldn't keep his cool but couldn't bring himself to do something about it. He looked like he might cry. That was answer enough. Dr. Pitchell had seen enough liars when this question came up and he knew there was truth here.

"I'm sorry, Cael, but I have to ask. I'm so sorry," Dr. Pitchell apologized. "Please, sit back down."

After a long silence, the doctor said: "What I think we should do is talk to Hailey together about this monster and see what she says. Perhaps your presence will comfort her enough to give more useful answers."

"I'd be happy to do that," Cael said, "just give me a minute."

"Of course."

Cael stood up and went to leave; he turned back to Dr. Pitchell as he opened the door to use the restroom.

"I just want my daughter to be my daughter again," he said.

* * *

They went into the small visiting room, Dr. Pitchell, Cael, and a nurse. Hailey came in a few minutes later with another nurse. Her long hair hung in her face and her pallid face was sickly against the bright blues of the walls. Cael tried to smile but thought he wasn't doing a very good job. This just tore him apart.

Everything was silent.

"Hi, honey," he finally said.

Hailey wasn't looking at him—she wasn't looking at anything. She was staring straight ahead, looking *through* everything, her hands up at her waist, about a foot apart. Dr. Pitchell said some things to her about her Daddy being there, but still there was nothing.

"Do you like what's in my box?"

The silence hung heavy in the air.

Hailey repeated flatly, "Do you like what's in my box?"

Now that he thought about it, it did look like she was miming a box, Cael thought bemusedly. No one said anything.

Again, her raspy little voice repeated, "Do you like what's in my box?"

"What's in your box?" Dr. Pitchell said.

In the same deadpan tone: "Do you like what's in my box?"

One of the nurses tried. "Hailey, what's in there? I can't see because your hands are blocking it."

Calmly, but firmer now: "Do you like what's in my box?"

"Yes, I do," Cael said as warmly as he could. "I like it a lot."

They all waited for Hailey to respond. Electricity crackled in the air. As if waking from a trance, Hailey put her invisible box on the floor and smiled. She looked up and when she saw her father her eyes brightened for the first time in many months. She ran over to him and gave him a hug.

"Daddy, come look," she said quickly. "Come and see where I've been playing!"

"Honey, we—"

"Come on!" she grabbed his arm and they ran for the door. The hospital staff followed. No one had seen Hailey this active since she came to Minaret. They were all secretly worried about what was going to happen. This kind of progress does not just happen immediately. Something was terribly wrong.

"Here's the TV area, and the dining room, and this is the kitchen set, and this is my drawing area, and..." it went on and on. Hailey was really just rambling off a list of toys and play areas, but as she talked her voice got stronger and more natural. She was in mid-sentence, telling them about the wonders inside the toy box when she suddenly stopped short and let out a scream so distraught and high-pitched only dogs could hear.

"Hailey! What's wrong?" Cael jumped, trying to grab her as she started to run away, screaming.

"It's here, Daddy! It's here!"

They all ran after her except for one nurse who went to the nurses' station to call security. All the other children looked around, some went back to their tasks with empty eyes, others stared, some began to cry. Cael paid them no attention. Hailey was running as fast as she could, sliding around turns and sprinting down the hallways. Cael was scared she would fling herself into a wall. This place was too small for her to run around like this. Eventually she ended up in the far bathroom. She stood against the back wall, shaking from fear, her eyes wide and chest heaving as she caught her breath.

Dr. Pitchell said, "Cael, keep her here. I'm going to get her some medicine before security gets here." He was off quickly.

"Daddy," Hailey begged—begged, deep from her chest, nearly sobbing—"Please, Daddy, make It go away! I don't want It to eat me tonight! Tell It that It can't have me, Daddy, *please!*"

He walked toward her cautiously, looking around. There was nothing there; there never had been.

"Honey, the monster's not here. You ran too fast. See? Look around, it's not here. You know I won't let anyone hurt you."

She screamed again, her eyes even wider, and bolted past him. She ran back the way she had come, then in and out of all the children's rooms, slamming doors open and shut. She was panicked. None of these rooms were safe.

Once she found her room Hailey sprang into the bed and quieted down quickly, pulling the pink flower-print covers around her, hiding her face. Cael looked at her from the doorway, his hands on the frame, catching his breath after fighting his emotions and chasing her. Her eyes were wide, red-rimmed, and fearful. They pleaded with him silently, filled deep with tears. She began to cry to herself, softly; it was more like a whimper than sobs but tears ran down her sallow cheeks. Her long black hair stuck to her face, tangled and thick from spit and snot. She turned her head away from him. He went to the bed hurriedly, ashamed that he wasn't already beside her. He tried his hardest to talk to her soothingly.

"Hailey, honey, what's the matter? Is. . .is it still the monster?"

He put his hand on her little shoulder to stroke her but she shrank away, as if his touch had hurt. He pulled his hand back reflexively; her reaction had scalded him. But it was more than that: she seemed so fragile now. Like even the softest touch would break her—like *he* was breaking her. That thought was too much and he brushed it away. She gave him no answer, just a timid moan.

"Hailey, baby, it's all right now…" his voice trailed off, unsure of where to go. "Uh…the monster is gone. Remember? We went into the bathroom and there was nothing there. It's not here now. Look for yourself."

It took a while, but she turned her head to face him, her big blue eyes swollen from tears. Cael was almost in tears himself; he could feel them trembling deep inside him, ready to come up. A million thoughts he couldn't place ran through his mind, terrible thoughts. He saw plainly all the confusion, hope, fear, and disappointment that looked at him from his daughter's saucer eyes.

"Daddy," she started, her voice cracking.

"What is it, baby? It's OK; you can tell me."

"It's…" you could hear the sobs in her voice, frightened and shallow.

"Hailey—"

"It's behind you, Daddy!" she shrieked.

As Cael turned he jumped before he could stop himself. In the doorway, watching them, was a Thing. *The* Thing Hailey had drawn and talked about. It was here, in front of them, snapping its… God, he didn't know what they were. He pushed himself back onto the bed and against the wall in one quick motion, grabbing Hailey and pulling her against his chest protectively, letting out a small yelp of fear involuntarily. Hailey was crying much harder now, shaking against him. The Thing stood there just staring at them. Feeling paralyzed in this dead room, trapped,

Cael could do nothing but stare back into those empty, fiery black holes.

It had the body of a man, but it was shiny and seemed scaled like a snake. Cael may have seen its long, fierce, disjointed claws, but he couldn't look away from its horrid face. Or, rather, Its lack of a face. Its large head was bald with muddied skin, red rings under its black eyes which were just hollow holes leading to nowhere, no nose—it was too horrible to imagine. Even worse and infinitely more frightening were its wicked yellow-brown teeth: jagged and offset three-inch fangs, tips bent inward and outward, crookedly fit together like protruding grating. They snapped together, quick and sharp.

Cael could swear that as It moved toward them, slowly, sneaking, It smiled.

3

It had been a year since the "incident" at Minaret, but Cael did not feel safe. He had lied about what happened that day; he said Hailey's fit, or tantrum, whatever you wanted to call it, had gotten him whipped up and he overreacted. Yes, screaming so loud it could be heard from the floor below was definitely an overreaction.

He told Hailey to lie to them; tell them what they wanted to hear, tell them the monster was gone, so that they could go home. He knew she wasn't safe there. He didn't know what the god-awful Thing in that room was, but he'd be damned if he let his daughter spend one more minute at that place.

It took six months before Dr. Pitchell released her. In those months, the monster had visited him—him, at his home—more times than he would ever admit. He would be getting dishes out of the cabinets or putting away groceries and when he shut the pantry door it would be there, at his side, staring at him, smiling that disgusting grin. He'd open his eyes in the shower after letting the hot, calming water stream down his face, trying to let it wash everything away, but it would be in front of him, teeth bared. Hailey said it left her alone most of the time but he didn't believe her. He had told her to lie to everyone else about it, so why wouldn't she lie to him?

Cael thought about moving them to a new house but knew the monster would follow them there. He knew it would never leave until it was dead. Or they were. He had never seen anything like that Thing, had never had anything like that happen to him before, but he knew he wasn't crazy and neither was his daughter. Something was going on here. He just needed to figure out what.

Hailey had begun talking to him in earnest again—really, she was back to her old self, or as much as a little girl who loses her mother, spends the better part of a year at a mental institution, and is haunted by visions can be. She played, ate and slept well, even laughed sometimes. Cael was very happy to see her improve and thrive. She would start school the next month, at the beginning of the new school year. She would repeat first grade at a new school because there had already been talk at her old school—talk about him, and his dead wife, but mostly about Hailey. There were rumors of neglect and abuse, he knew, but nothing had ever actually been said to his face. No Family Services agents rang his doorbell.

Maybe putting Hailey in a mental institution was evidence enough of a problem.

But they were getting better now, the two of them, and things were going to continue to improve. They were going to keep smiling and laughing and they would forget about that Thing that would stand in their doorways at night, its long, thin tongue slowly licking its fangs. He would forget about the Thing that would reach for him out of the darkness, its claws hooked on the ends of long slender fingers, the knuckles hard, large, and bony. Things would get better, he knew.

He hoped.

* * *

On Saturday they went to the store to buy Hailey's school supplies. She had decided to go with a pink polka dot backpack, and folders covered with flowers and hearts instead of the popular television character line of products. Secretly Cael was glad: he had seen that show, and it was terrible. He knew children's shows were supposed to be corny, but that show was almost too much. Yes, its teenaged female lead was good, and an ok singer, and she was probably a good role model, but he didn't want his daughter to be wearing her face all the time. He was very pleased that she had gone with something girly and was excited for school.

Traffic was better than what a Saturday afternoon should have been, but there were still plenty of cars on the road with them. Hailey was rambling away in the backseat, jabbering about "what ifs:" what if dogs could drive cars? What if we could get into a giant spaceship and fly to planets and meet aliens? What if hot dogs were made of bananas? What if everyone turned into monkeys? They laughed together at the silly things, hard laughing, the kind that brings tears to your eyes and releases all bad energy from you. Luckily while he laughed hardest they were at a stoplight because Cael might have wrecked the car. When the light turned green, Cael noticed that the same type of car, same color even, as their own was next to them.

When Cael looked at the driver, it was him. He was crying, but not from laughing. He quickly turned to look in the backseat of the other car; Hailey was not there. He looked again: yes, he was the driver in that car. He started to ask Hailey if she saw it too, but cars started honking behind him. He slowly rolled forward, constantly looking at the car beside them. It was rolling forward too. Suddenly, the red SUV that was right behind them whipped into the other lane and passed them. It drove through the car Cad had seen himself in, like passing through vapor. The car was gone now. Had it even really been there?

4

Fire is sacred. It burns away without restraint and reduces everything to ash. Ashes to ashes, dust to dust. Fire brings change. It is a chemical reaction—perfectly natural, just heat and need. The need to purge all the blackness into light: orange and yellow, red and blue. Just take a match and scrape the sulfur, phosphorous, and glass powder against any surface and watch it spark to life. It will inhale precious oxygen and then you can watch it rampage. Watch it, consider it, feel it, want it, need it.

All it takes is one match, Samuel thought as his eyes wandered over the matchbox in his right hand. He held it between his first two fingers and thumb, turning it in a circle with dull taps against the kitchen table. He lightly pushed his ring finger and pinkie against his palm, just enough pressure to keep him grounded. He needed to remember the reality of his situation.

He closed his eyes and tried not to remember; he tried not to think. Let the blackness come and have some peace.

It didn't work.

When his eyelids snapped open to reveal the gray eyes underneath, wide and sullen, they immediately focused on the table. This was not his kitchen anymore. This house held nothing for him any more but memories he wished he could forget. He had tried pills, alcohol, therapy—anything to make the memories end. Nothing worked.

He had been up for 42 hours straight. It was 2am and it felt like all his nerves were exposed, as if they stuck out of his pores like blackheads. The air in the house, this dead monument to his misery, was stale and sticky. He could feel the electricity pulsing in the walls around him and it made him nervous. He had been nervous for a long time, and been crying for even longer.

As he stared at the kitchen sink, he second-guessed himself again and decided to take a shower. Maybe the hot water would open his mind and take away this absolute feeling of…tired. He was just so tired.

The water had steamed the mirror and hung in the air almost like fog, thick and gray. Samuel held his hands in front of him and watched as the water slipped through his fingers, overflowed from his palm, and hit the bottom of the floor to explode like his tears exploded on his cheeks, scalding reminders. Everywhere around him were reminders of what his life had been before the monsters came in. Memories of wandering stars passing by his window at night while he watched Maria sleep; memories of long nights on the couch watching movies, doubled over in laughter; haunting memories of the warmth of her skin, the scent of her hair, the way she looked at him. He turned around in the shower and saw where they had carved their names and a heart into the wall after a particularly wild night of sex. They had wanted everyone who lived in this house after them to know how much they loved each other. He could still see her in the shower with him, her brown hair slicked to her oval face, steam around her like a fog. When he remembered her he thought of an angel coming out of the fog, his angel.

But now she was dead, and when she died he had as well.

He knew what he was about to do was wrong, that he should just sleep it off. But his mind would not stop now, and he could not control it. Long ago he had resigned to the fact that his madness was beyond redemption. There were no pills that could fix him, no self-help book, no therapist, no song, no movie, no beautiful spring day to lift his spirits; there were no means of escape.

There was only the need to end that unending, aching need.

He turned off the shower, dried off, put on some boxers and went back to the kitchen. He drank one last diet Dr. Pepper, his favorite, picked up his box of matches, and then went into the garage. There were three containers of gasoline on the floor. He took each one separately and flooded the house with it; soaked it into the carpets and filled the sinks, covered the beds.

And then he poured it over himself, choking against its stench. *This is it*, he thought. And then, more urgently, *it will all be over*.

He lay down on the bed, closed his stinging eyes, breathed in that acrid smell, three long, deep, controlled breaths, and then, before he watched his hands, almost out-of-body, pick out one match, he prayed. He needed someone to know he could not stop himself and that he was sorry. He was so, so sorry that he could not make himself better, that he had not been a better person, that he was such a bitter disappointment. He was bitter, and beyond miserable. Samuel prayed for his soul, and he prayed hard for forgiveness because it was too late now and he thought maybe, just maybe, repentance could save his immortal soul. Watching his fingers put pressure against the sandpaper of the box, he could not look away. He wanted to see. If nothing else, he needed to know that he had done it. There could be no waking up.

He saw the spark that ended his life.

5

"Let me out!"

The voice coming from the darkness was normal, like a teenager's; it seemed to be coming from the bushes outside. They had grown incredibly fast, Cael noticed, much too fast for autumn. The nature outside his window was turning into deep reds, like blood, and oranges, like fire, but this bush was dying as well. It was shriveling up, its braches no longer covered in needles but bare, knotted bones. It had become a chaotic mass that somehow grew noticeably taller by the day.

Every night, as he began to doze, his mind on the expansive threshold of sleep, the voice would emerge from the dark: "Let me out."

Cael decided tonight was the night to do something about it. He didn't care if he sounded crazy; this had to stop. He had to do something. He couldn't go on like this one night longer. He pulled back the covers and reluctantly walked toward the window. Without looking at the bush, he said, cautiously, "Hello?"

"Let me out!" the voice yelled, without missing a beat. "I can't get out of here! You have to help me!"

Cael took a step closer to the window. He looked outside. There was no one there.

"Where are you?" he asked. His voice was shaky. Was he really talking to the air?

"I don't know where I am—I can see a big tree and the siding of this house. I can't see anything else. Where am I?"

Cael looked down. The voice was definitely coming from the bush.

"You're in the bush outside my house. You're—you're a bush."

"What?"

The bush was confused. Cael laughed to himself. He was talking to a bush, trying to explain something to it. If it were burning this would be hysterical: Cael, seer of visions, of demons, talking to a burning bush. He put on his bathrobe and went outside. The bush was thorny and gnarled; it looked like a possessed bush should.

"My name is Cael, and for the last two weeks you've been calling out into the darkness for me."

"Where is your house?" The voice no longer sounded like a teenager's, it was grittier, but still a young voice.

Cael told him where he lived. The bush was silent. The still air around them seemed stagnant, like the crickets were waiting for their moment to chirp.

Finally, the bush said: "My name is Samuel. I—" there was a slight hesitation—"I know about you and your daughter."

Cael could not speak. The bush began to move its branches, slowly, as if to try and untie them.

"How do you know about—"

""Hailey? I know all about Hailey, and her visions, and that you've seen It as well. You've both seen *Him*."

At mentioning of it, Cael could see the Thing in his head. He

37

hadn't seen the Creature for a while, and felt blessedly rid of it. In his mind he saw It sitting in the tree behind him, in the high red leaves, licking its horrid lips, blood dripping down Its chin.

"I've seen Him too," the bush offered.

"When? Where?" Cael asked. His mind offered up a million questions but could only voice two.

"I…"

He—the Thing—It—climbed out of the tree and stepped into Cael's view. He snapped his head to look at It but It was gone. The bush continued.

"…I killed myself. My girlfriend died and I burned my house down while I was inside it. I woke up, started screaming. Then He called to me, almost like the words had been put straight into my mind. His claws were scratching the walls; pieces of it flaking into the air and floating around like an ashen wind. I think He had been waiting for me all along."

"Where were you?"

"Hell."

Cael didn't know what to say. The answer had been so matter-of-fact. *Hell.*

"Why are you here? Why didn't He keep you—there?"

"Because my soul, and the other souls he already claimed, are not enough. All He really wants is you, but your will is very strong. He has always wanted you but you resisted. So He tried to take your daughter. Her will is strong as well, I'm afraid."

"Why are you afraid?"

"The longer you deny Him the worse it will be. The longer you resist, the harder He will have you."

"Have me?"

"He will take you places you have never been—to the most horrid, marvelous place you could ever imagine. If you'll just let Him in, let Him take you, and Hailey, if you wish, it will be ecstasy,

I promise." Samuel's voice had become honeyed, like the thought itself was pleasurable.

"I thought you were in hell."

"I was."

"Ecstasy in hell? I don't buy it." Cael began to laugh, almost uncontrollably, at the scene: he was talking to a bush, yet he doubted what it had to say.

The voice boomed from knotted branches: "Silence!"

Cael did as he was ordered.

"I am trying to tell you something very important," Samuel said. "I am stuck here, in this plant, until you give up. And you will give up, I assure you. The sooner you do it the better off you will be. If you do not surrender to your mind—I know you can feel His grip even now—then He will take no pity on you. I have seen what He can do; I have seen Him tear open flesh with his whip-tongue, and wait for the wounds to heal so He can slice them open again. I have seen Him tie boulders to a child's back, and then laugh when she smothered in the dirt. Your daughter will have much worse, no doubt."

"I'm not going to listen to this," Cael said, and walked back inside. The bush called after him, its voice hoarse and pleading. It cursed warnings at him, but Cael shut them out. He returned to his bedroom, shut and locked the window, and went to check on Hailey.

Hell, ecstasy beyond his wildest dreams, torn flesh, talking bushes—he really was going crazy.

* * *

Cael opened the door to Hailey's room slowly, trying not to wake her. As the door passed him, heat hit his face in a wave. He stumbled backward, and saw her room was on fire.

No, not on fire: through squinted eyes he could see the dresser was still in one piece, as was her bed, and her toys still lined the ground, looking at him with smiling eyes. Hailey's room was not on fire, but it was no longer her room. It was in a tunnel of fire, an eternal tunnel; he could hear her screaming for him. From somewhere deep in the void her voice rose, a high timber, that begged for her Daddy.

Cael jumped over the bed and ran into the tunnel. The ground was like a sewer, its putrid smell burning his nostrils, and the flames licked his flesh. He ran for almost a mile, panting, his adrenaline high, running toward Hailey's voice. Abruptly the tunnel opened to another tunnel on the right and he followed it. He stopped as soon as he turned.

This, without a doubt, was hell.

The air itself seemed sorrowed, full of smoke and cries. There was a woman with her eyes and mouth sewn shut, naked, crawling toward him, trying to feel her way out. Cael backed away from her, repulsed. He backed into a wall. The tunnel had closed; this hallway was not endless. It was stopped, like a giant stone had been rolled in front of it. He was trapped. When she was within three feet of him, He came for her.

It had crawled out from under the wall. Or, rather, it slid out, on the air; it rose like a cloud of glossy skin and molded back into its lizard-man shape. Its teeth had grown by at least three inches. His claws had the same. He grabbed the woman's tight flesh with its claws, impaled her back with the spikes, and dragged her into a far corner Cael could not see. He could hear, however, her heart pumping. He knew it was her heart, beating faster and faster, louder and louder, until it must burst, and then there was silence. He appeared again, blood smeared across His face, smiling.

Hailey was in His arms.

She looked like she was sleeping; in fact, she seemed to be at peace. Her long black hair was wrapped around the Thing's arms like rope. The Thing walked toward him, slowly, carrying his daughter, and Cael looked away. He could not bear to see his daughter slaughtered.

Cael's mind spoke to him: *Don't look away. She is fine.*

Confused, Cael opened his eyes. They widened when he realized It was talking to him, inside his head. It sounded like the voice of an old friend. It was comforting, and in that split second Cael was no longer afraid. He turned to face It.

You have been very strong, my dear, but you can never be stronger than Me. Look at your daughter's sweet face—do you want me to suck her eyes out? I would like that very much. Or I could bury her alive, up to her neck in this sewer-soil, and let the dogs eat her. They are very hungry.

Its black tomb of a face seemed to expand into a vacuum that stretched right to Cael's mind. They were connected, invisibly, and Cael could not help but listen. Indeed, he found he wanted to listen.

I tell you again, she will not be hurt. I will spare her, and she will remain in this sleep, if you give to me what is rightfully mine.

Cael didn't know what the Thing meant.

It continued, poised, as if it had been practicing this for years: *I am the nightmare you saw as a child, the monster under the bed, if you will. I am the snake that bit you at seventeen on that camping trip, the venom that poisoned your mind. I am that aching sadness within you made flesh. I cannot be without you any longer. I have existed for so long, here in this carnage, with only half a heart. You are the other half of misery, and I need to be put together again. I have waited so long for you, Caleb, so long.*

My name is Cael.

No, my love, your name is Caleb Sampson. You gave yourself to me as a boy, full heartedly, but then you escaped me. You grew into a man—a fine man, I must say, I am proud of you—but you can never really escape.

My name is Cael.

No. *You* know *me, boy.*

It spoke truth.

You cannot live without me for too much longer, so it is no use to refuse. You have always been mine and you always will. I own your brain, I own your soul. Caleb, you cannot escape me, like you did that night at the hospital. There is nowhere to run to. Give yourself to me, fully, like you did before.

It reached out to him with its twisted hands, and asked: *Shall I take her too?*

"No," Caleb answered. "Leave her be."

And with that, Hailey disappeared, and Caleb did not even know it. He forgot his past, the lie he had made himself, and became that scared little boy.

"Who are you?" he asked.

I am sadness. I am regret. I am what your medicine can never cure. There is no pill to wipe my stain away. You can never wash my stink off. I am your sadness, your agony; I am you.

Caleb understood, and walked, in airplane pajamas, to himself. The Thing withered, its skin wrinkling and pulled like an old woman's and then shrinking to nothing. Caleb felt it go into his stomach. It pitted itself there, shook his core, and then rose out of him. It came up his throat like vomit and as it spewed from his mouth it took shape again, this time Its eyes bright.

It spread its teeth wide, and this head, all the horrors of Caleb's own mind, ate him whole.

Masked Death

D eath wears a mask that looks like your face. It is pieced together in skin and bone. When Death comes for kings, he wears a mask of gold with ruby eyes of the finest sheen. When he comes for the weak his face is angled and strong. The sick are greeted with the skull they will soon leave.

Death is no respecter of persons; he may come for any one at any time. When he is needed, his scythe fingers will slit throats. His breath will freeze the heart and his voice burst the brain. Death can be an angel, a great mercy, or indisputable agony.

When Death came for Eliza Lovejoy, he was in a grand mood, and decided to play a game.

* * *

The Death and Dying exhibit had nearly reached its end at the Thomas Brown Museum when Eliza first explored it. It was extra credit for her anthropology class, and after her last test Eliza needed all the help she could get. The assignment was to peruse the displays and write a one-page reflective essay on the many faces of death.

The tribal portion of the exhibit intrigued Eliza the most; the outrageous costumes, in graphic detail, were fascinating. She also enjoyed the artifacts and demonstrations of cultures that celebrate death; it was so wonderfully exotic for her to see the passing of a loved one commemorated rather than mourned. As she roamed the long hallways, most of them dimly lit, Eliza discovered new fascinations around every corner, new treasures to be examined. She was very analytical; her thinking was precise. Death was philosophical and her brain had trouble processing it—the straightforward presentation of the exhibits helped her.

At the end of a back hallway, too far away from all the other exhibits, Eliza thought, was a collection of death masks. She knew these were fairly common; she had seen John Keats' death mask more than she would have liked in her English Literature class. But there were replicas of other famous faces, like Queen Elizabeth I and Abraham Lincoln, which she thought were pretty cool. Eliza scanned the shelves face by face, reading all the details about each mask. It was increasingly morbid to note how many times the death masks seemed to be smiling.

The middle mask on the second to last shelf was not smiling, however. Its face seemed twisted in pain and the eyes looked like they were open. When she saw it, Eliza threw up, right on the floor.

The pained face was her own.

There was no mistaking it: she knew her own face. Seeing her face countless times in the mirror or in pictures she undoubtedly knew it was hers. All of the details were there; there was even a small raised knot above the left eyebrow where she had a scar from a bicycle accident in seventh grade. As she wiped off her mouth, Eliza looked at the death mask again, certain her eyes would see someone else, maybe Mary, Queen of Scots, or even Ben Franklin.

Eliza's death mask screamed back at her in white, mute agony.

* * *

"Maybe you just imagined it, you know?" her roommate, Molly, told her. "Surrounded by all that death imagery—your mind can play tricks on you."

"I know what I saw," Eliza kept repeating. She had been saying this simple phrase for the last hour. Neither Molly nor her own boyfriend, Landon, believed her. They thought she had simply daydreamed it; her inspired mind was playing out some elaborate scheme, some funny trick.

Eliza did not get the joke.

She ended up blowing off both Landon and Molly and went to bed before she had even eaten dinner, in mid-evening. She knew she had seen her own death mask. She just had to prove it. She made up her mind to take both doubters to the museum the next day and prove them wrong.

Death, waiting in the corners of Eliza's room, watching her, smiled. She had taken the bait with more intensity than he had anticipated. Seeing her squirm like this was excruciatingly fun. He made his way back to the museum to retrieve his mask. He had a few more tricks to pull.

* * *

The game was simple: to see how long it would take for Eliza to break. Death had played this sport many times; each participant had broken quickly. He was certain Eliza would need some coaxing. He asked his friends for assistance, to make the session as slow and pleasurable as possible.

First, he enlisted Albatross. Always a faithful servant, Albatross was more of a mind-trick than actual helper in this game. His job was to perch on rooftops and street lamps since his form resembled a gargoyle. At night, his stature was quite terrifying. He was to exist in Eliza's peripheral vision for three days, and then, only on day four, was he allowed to show his hideous glory.

Eliza didn't even notice Albatross until day four. She had taken Molly and Landon to the museum, but her death mask was nowhere to be found. They searched every side exhibit, every crack and corner, but came up empty. Molly, ever the supportive friend, stayed in the search longer than Landon, whose easily flared temper was already sparking.

"Told you," was all he would say. He left quickly and tromped to the car, bored that he had even entertained the idea of finding the mask.

Eventually, Molly left too. She didn't have anything to say.

Albatross followed Eliza, perched on rooftops, car tops, treetops, chimneys, anywhere he could find purchase, but was not noticed. Finally, after a fight with Landon, who thought Eliza was going crazy—"just a little. I mean, c'mon Liza! This is too much"—she emerged from her apartment building. Needing a bit of refreshment, she took in a deep breath of the crisp air, feeling it clear her mind. When she opened her eyes, she expected to see a sunny display on the shingles of the laundry mat (they always sparkled in the sun, like they were covered in glitter), she instead saw Albatross.

Death had given one rule: do not show yourself until the fourth day. Death knew Albatross enjoyed his body and took delight in flaunting it, but he would have to wait or pay the consequences. You do not want to face Death's consequences. So Albatross went unseen until Eliza looked at the Laundromat. When she saw him, she was confused—he looked like some strange statue. Then he stood up.

The Albatross was large, so large, in fact, that his legs could never be seen, his girth covered them, and completely black. Its feathers had a slight sheen, but were frayed, which gave him a disheveled look. As he rose from his crouch he spread his six wings, all hooked at 90-degree angles. He flapped a few times, puffed out his chest, and turned so Eliza could see his face. What Eliza beheld was not a face but a cranium fronted with nothing but a giant beak, like an eagle's but smooth and black like onyx. The Albatross had no eyes—Death had given him sight without burdensome sockets.

As Eliza looked at the phoenix from hell across the street, she did not even register what was happening. Her mind fled from the occurrence with tremendous force; that same force hit her chest when her mind came back to her and she knew this apparition was real. She stumbled backward and fell into the hedges; she rolled onto her hands and knees and crawled up the front steps, her mouth agape. At the same instant she dropped her keys onto the concrete with a *clink* as she tried to unlock the door, the Albatross leapt from the gutter. It flew at her and swooped down as if to pick her up in its gigantic claws, but did not. Instead, it flew back home, pleased with the fear it had seen in her eyes. Death would be pleased as well, he knew, and looked forward to his reward.

Eliza retrieved her keys and ran back upstairs to her apartment. At first Landon thought someone had tried to attack her. His male mind prepared itself to go outside, find that man, and kick some ass. But when Eliza's babbling became coherent, his stomach dropped.

As he walked out of the apartment, shaking his head, to Eliza's frightened tears he whispered: "My girlfriend is a fucking lunatic."

* * *

Harlequin and Candystriper were next. They had been in Death's service for many centuries and knew what needed to be done as soon as they were summoned. Death would set the bait, and, having effectively scared the shit out of Eliza, would lead her to Harlequin. Harlequin would take Eliza to the bowels of the earth where Candystriper lived. He would then bring Eliza to Death for the grand finale, fireworks and all, as they say.

That bait was an article in the next day's newspaper:

UNIDENTIFIED DEATH MASK STOLEN FROM THOMAS BROWN MUSEUM

The article was bare-bones. It did, however, confirm Eliza's story, without actually saying it. This, of course, was acknowledged by Landon, who rightfully said that just because *a* death mask of a young woman was stolen, that doesn't necessarily mean it was *her* mask. If her mask had even really existed, he thought.

In the face of doubt from Landon and Molly, the only two people in the world Eliza had, she decided not to go to the police. They wouldn't have believed her anyway. She tried to decide what to do: ignore it, or go back to the exhibit; she couldn't stop thinking that the museum was tied into all this. That and the black atrocity that she had narrowly escaped from.

Instead of Eliza finding the next piece of the puzzle, the puzzle came to her.

To clear her head, Eliza sat on the roof of her apartment building. She just sat and thought. She tried to relax, to enjoy the sunny day, but couldn't. After fifteen failed minutes she went back down to her apartment.

As she was descending, from a side hallway a woman emerged, stopping right in front of her. This woman was big—and not because of weight, but her dress. She was in a pink Victorian ball gown, but it was tattered at the hem and soiled, like soot and dirt had been rubbed into it; the sleeves were short and puffed, and she had on elbow-length once-white gloves that now were a dingy yellow. The collar of her dress was high and squared, like the slant of the black bird's wings, but they were sheer and glossy, like an insect's wings. On closer inspection, the veins of the winged collar looked not like veins, but tiny bones—children's bones. Her hair, the same shiny black as the bird from the day before, was pulled up in a bun like a geisha. Eliza's first thought was that she actually was a geisha, in some displaced reality, because of her hair and her pale face. Then, she saw that the woman's dress and gloves were actually sewn to her skin with thread that was unmistakably rope, edged with crusted blood.

The woman had cut Eliza off and stood in profile to her. When she turned, to show herself, the face was Eliza's: her death mask, with its lips painted a thick and lumpy maroon. The eyes had been painted over with two giant, black X's.

Eliza screamed. She screamed not out of fright, but anger. All her confusion and fear mixed into a knot of hate and Eliza screamed like she had never screamed before, from a place deep inside her, under her stomach, at her core. At the scream, Harlequin did not jump, or run. She simply looked at Eliza with a cocked head, and turned around gingerly, daintily picking up her skirt. She then proceeded down the stairs.

Eliza ran after her, taking the stairs two, three at a time—but Harlequin somehow was always just out of reach. It seemed the faster Eliza ran, the longer her opponent's strides became, although she exerted much less effort. Eventually, they had passed the ground level of the building and headed down into the basement—and then, before Eliza noticed, down even farther.

They entered a labyrinth, a boxed maze with rusted stone walls and hard dirt floors. At every turn, they went deeper and deeper down, Harlequin striding along, Eliza panting. In her heat Eliza had not recognized that she was no longer in her apartment building; her focus had become tunneled. She only snapped back into herself when the maze abruptly ended and Harlequin disappeared.

Eliza looked around for the woman wearing her face, but she had vanished. Something else stepped into view, something big. It was a giant, at least nine feet tall, in green corduroy overalls. Eliza scanned up its body, her stomach turning as her body grasped what she was seeing before her mind did.

The thing's skin was wrong. No, there could be no skin like this: it was twisted around, like it was subject to a perpetual Indian rug burn. But where the skin should have split, or bled, instead it just lapped over, until it spiraled, deep tan and varicose purple-red. If this were not horrible enough, the skin was not just twisted on the thing's arms—its chest was warped as well. Then, Eliza saw with horror, that its face was twisted. Its lips were entwined together, one grotesque pink tangle, forked tongue hanging limply out toward the left. Its nose was just a lump in the middle of the bald head. Its eyes were twisted as well, sticking out an inch from the skull, the lavender irises bisected by lashes and thin skin. The eyes moved, the whole ball, eyelid included, in unison. They looked from side to side before finally dipping down to look into Eliza's terrified face.

When the thing touched her, Eliza fainted.

* * *

Candystriper took this deliciously lean piece of meat to its master, and like a good dog, he sat it at Death's feet and retrieved his reward. Then he galloped away to go play with the other toys Death had recently brought home.

Once the waves of sleep receded from Eliza's mind she got to her feet and realized she was shackled to the ground. Her left foot was attached to a cast iron cuff and chain that resisted her movement like it was stuck into the middle of the world. She could not escape. Her death mask, freshly cleaned, lay next to her.

"Hello, Eliza," a high-pitched, shrill voice said to her. She looked around but could not find the source of the sound. Then a black shape emerged in the air, like a swarm of gnats that grew and grew until it was solid; from this a black cloak formed. Eliza knew who was underneath—its scythe fingertips were unmistakable.

"You must be Death," she replied, trying her best to sound brave.

"Yes, I am," the almost-feminine voice replied.

"Can I ask you something?"

"Of course."

"What the hell is going on?"

Death laughed from its chest, an open, echoing sound, that was no longer delicate but a million jumbled cries.

"You see, this is why I chose you. I knew you wouldn't disappoint. This will be ever so much fun," Death said. "I will enjoy taking you."

"So you're going to kill me."

"Not quite. You will die, but I will not *murder* you. I entertain no malice."

Eliza cut him off: "Then what?"

"You have been called for. However, I am willing to strike a bargain, if you wish to keep your skin."

Eliza's eyebrows furrowed and she looked away from the cloaked figure. She had heard of Death bargaining with his victims, but had never heard of anyone actually winning. Everyone dies.

"What are your terms?"

Death laughed again, this time a seething chuckle.

"So far you have proven quite resilient. You were more intrigued than anything else when you saw this mask I made. I have a collection, you see. Then, you were scared, but not damaged, by my Albatross bird. In fact, you made him quite angry; he followed you around for three days before you noticed him. Harlequin lured you here, and delivered you to Candystriper, my pet. He brought you to me. Throughout all of this, you have kept your head. My test is to see if you can stand seeing mine."

"What do you mean?"

"If you can look at my face, you may live. If not, you are mine."

Eliza laughed.

"That's it? I just have to look at you."

The voice became stern, like a rasp: "Do not underestimate me, child. I have played this game many times before, and no one has ever won." As an afterthought, he added, "I don't cheat."

"Now," Death continued, "I am a fair man. I will not scare you with a sudden revelation or disfigure myself in any way. Instead, I shall take off my hood and you will see your death, for I do not have a soul of my own. Is this acceptable to you?"

Eliza thought for a long time about what she should do, knowing she must accept or her death be immediate. She tried to prepare herself for the worst, but a part of her knew that if his pets were any clue, his face would be terrible. Shouldn't the face of Death disgust? Why would it invite?

"I accept."

Death extended a bony claw, and, like a true gentleman said, "Shall we?"

Stone benches appeared behind them and they each took their seat.

The skeleton hand gently grabbed its hood and lowered it, very slowly, its eyes downcast. At first, there was nothing. Then, black and blond matted hair was revealed, followed by rusted-looking flesh. Eliza could see bits of skin were hanging off the skull, her body already decomposed.

"Are you ready to see more?" Eliza's own voice asked her.

"Yes."

Slowly the head rose and Eliza saw with terror that her entire face was rotted and black. Her eyes were missing, and in their place lay hundreds of wriggling maggots. The tip of her nose was gone, replaced by a large chunk of roots from the dirt. The remnants of her mouth were, as her death mask portrayed, drawn up in a grimacing scream. Some of her teeth were missing; others were stained and chipped. All of the veins in her face were exposed through her thin skin. One of the maggots fell onto Eliza's lap. She flinched, but was not afraid.

"How do I die?" she managed to ask, her voice weak.

"A car accident—a driver on a cell phone. Very messy."

"And this is what happens to me?"

Her decrepit mouth spoke to her, worms spilling out, "The car burns while you are trapped inside. Your nose is crushed by the airbag. In addition, both your legs are broken and one of your ribs punctures your lung. You will die before the emergency crews can rescue you from the burning car."

Eliza looked at herself, disgusted, her heart in her throat. As her dead body spoke to her she could feel the blow of the airbag and the stab of bone into flesh.

"May I ask you something else?" Eliza was not sure she wanted to ask at all, but her mouth moved before she could stop it.

"Anything."

"When?"

"About six years from now. You will leave behind a job as a pediatrician, a grieving husband, and a bouncing baby boy."

"I'm going to have children?"

"Before you die, just one. Perhaps there could have been more; who knows? What I can tell you is that you do not have to face any of this. You can die, right now, asleep in your apartment, or you can burn alive. The choice is yours."

Eliza said, without hesitation, "No."

"No?"

Eliza shook her head, her blond bangs falling into her eyes. She thought about her eyes being devoured by maggots, and her beautiful hair singed and matted with blood.

"I am going to need more than that," Death said. "No—you do not want this, or no—you do not wish to die?"

"I do not wish to die."

"You would burn alive, in pain and terror?"

"To experience love and have a child—yes, I would. Just to feel one moment with my husband, or hear my baby's voice: I would burn a million times for that."

Death nodded. "There is much pain in your future, some nasty heartbreak, some terrible failures."

"I'll deal with it," Eliza replied.

With that, Death replaced his hood and snapped his joints. The chain on Eliza's ankle disintegrated.

Eliza could hear Molly laughing with Landon. When they

heard her shuffle about, Landon came to the doorway. He smiled at her with a look in his eyes that Eliza had not seen since their first date.

"Want to go see that death exhibit at the museum before it closes?" he asked her.

Silence and Rage

Kim Fehr was all alone, again. As she sat on the edge of her bed, studying her newest music magazines inside her calculus book, she was utterly alone. She thought of no one and she was reasonably sure no one was thinking of her. And that was just fine. In fact, if there was someone out there in that big, big world that had her on his mind, she pitied him. There was no real reason to think of her. After all, she wasn't anything special.

But across the street, staring out of a second-story window, James Richardson was gorging on thoughts of Kim. There was no way he couldn't be: binoculars don't lie.

Actually, it was hard for him to tell exactly what he was thinking. Lately, whenever he thought of Kim—his beauty, his love, his only—his brain turned inside-out. Everything dissolved and meshed together into one big confusion. He shook his head roughly, trying to clear his thoughts. It didn't work. All it did was add a throbbing stab of pain to the clutter.

He wondered if maybe Kim wasn't the best person to admire. If this was going to work, he needed to be clear-headed. He couldn't get caught up in anything. He had to keep his nose to the grindstone and take care of business. Failure was not an option, and his questioned if his—admiration—for Kim would cloud his judgment. Because if it did he would fail, that would be a great shame: over two and a half years' work down the drain.

But that wouldn't happen. This was going to work. It *had* to work. He wasn't going to screw things up in any way, because he was well prepared. That was why this whole thing had taken three years in the first place.

Kim shut her calculus book suddenly and it startled him. He squinted behind the binoculars. His mind cleared. He got back his focus. Kim dropped the book on the floor and climbed up her bed, that wasteland of mismatched pillows, sheets, and blankets. She lay on her back, her hands supporting her head. James looked at her body, eyes slowly roaming over her tight T-shirt; he wondered what she was thinking about.

He was enthralled.

The two stayed stationary for what seemed like forever.

Kim was thinking about her English assignment and how she was going to pull off writing a six-page paper at the last minute. It wouldn't be that hard—she'd written longer with less preparation and gotten A's. She'd be fine. As long as it was English, not math or science that she was blowing off, she'd pass with ease.

James was thinking about Kim, as usual. She'd fully occupied his thoughts for quite a while now. At first it was just infatuation, but then it started to grow. Now she *consumed* him. He was convinced that she was everything he had ever wanted. But no one saw that. All the "general yuppies," as he liked to call them, saw was a slightly-pretty, but could use some work, brainy, comical, lively girl. But that wasn't what James saw. He saw a gorgeous, intelligent, hilarious, thought provoking, talented, well-spoken girl who lit up his life. She was, well, perfect. She was absolutely *perfect*. And she would make him the happiest man alive.

He could see it now: their wedding. Thousands were in

attendance. There were flowers, lace, glitter, and love in abundance. Photographers crammed the doorways and were lining the streets just to get a glimpse of the mind-blowing spectacle inside. The bell outside the church shuddered three times, and then she appeared.

There she was—the most beautiful woman in the world. Her white dress clung to her body and flaunted it in just the right places. Her long brown hair flowed over her shoulders. A veil covered her dazzling face, which was a little disappointing, and her head was crowned with white roses.

And, best of all, she was smiling at him.

She loved him more than she loved anything or anyone else. He was somebody to her. He *mattered* now. It was a nice change.

She walked toward him. The closer she got the bigger her smile. And then, in a flash, she was there, standing right in front of him—his bride, his prize—and she was smiling at him. That smile that melted every inch of him. It was glowing just for him, for him and him only. She pulled back her veil and winked at him. She leaned closer. She was going to kiss him. She—

Kim's mother called to her from downstairs. Kim hopped off her bed and trotted out of the room.

James Richardson was all alone, again. Kneeling in front of the window of a bare second-story room, he was utterly alone. And that was *not* all right.

* * *

The strangest form of anticipation and fear was upon him as he stood in front of her house. He had been planning this moment for so long and now he was actually doing it. He was going to make his move. He felt paralyzed somewhat, as much by the expectations he had and what would happen if he was let down as much as he was by sheer adrenaline. He wanted to move, but couldn't. He was terrified. His mind was full of white noise. His mind *was* white noise. But he was here. He was actually *making his move*—the first move, the hardest one.

He walked into the house. The lock was not a problem; the Fehrs kept an extra key two feet from the door, under the barbecue. It was easy to find. A little too easy, he thought, but it was nice—he was most frightened that they would hear him coming in. But they didn't. He knew they didn't have an alarm, so that was good, another worry he could strike from his list. He listened to make sure none of them were stirring, and once he was satisfied, he shifted forward. Now that he knew he could get in undetected a whole new world opened up for him. He had access to *everything*. He could have them, any one of them, whenever he wanted. They were there for the taking whenever it struck his fancy. This was too good to be true. But here he was, standing in their living room.

The room was decidedly bare. There was an overstuffed chair in the corner directly to his right, and a small table with a lamp on it stood close by. Along the right wall, right where the living room met the kitchen, was a piano. Kim had been playing since she was six. He knew that. He laughed to himself. He knew everything there was to know. He knew things *she* didn't even know. The piano was big, but nothing impressive. He made a mental note to get a better one for Kim when the time came. Along the left wall was a couch, all by its lonesome. Other than that, the room was empty.

The carpet was light, gray. The same carpet covered the entire house, save the kitchen. Well, the entire house save the kitchen and Kim's room. Kim's room had blue carpet. She wanted black, but her parents were adamant that she not have black. Their defense had been that it would get dirty too easily and be more work for Kim because she would have to vacuum it all the time.

Try and get your way by implying extra work to your teenager. James shook his head. Kim was no ordinary teenager, and she wouldn't have minded the work. She had more responsibility in her little finger than both her parents' entire bodies had put together. He knew the real reason they wouldn't let her have black carpet was because they thought it was a little demonic. Their little girl *could not* be dark, no matter how much she wanted to be. No, no, no. They always said that. No, no, no.

James knew he would never deny Kim of anything, ever. Except, of course, if she wanted to leave him. But she wouldn't. He'd make sure of that.

The day the blue carpet was installed James had his entire house carpeted black. She would love that. He knew she would. He could feel it now as he explored the house. She would be so happy with him.

He would be happy, *finally*, thanks to Kim.

And because that was so imperative he did everything he could to make her "new station" exactly what she wanted. When the time came, she would love her "new station." And he would love her, unconditionally.

The house wasn't extravagant, mostly because the Fehrs had a lot of debt, and they weren't going to waste what little money they had on making their house *hospitable*. It was cold, sanitary, to the point, almost militant, James thought. There was no room for creativity or happiness here. There was love in this house, but not enough, and it was not given freely. No wonder Kim hated it so much. Well, he was reasonably sure Kim hated it. He did—mostly because he wasn't there.

He decided to explore the first floor.

Standing on the edge of the living room, to his right was the kitchen. It had black and white checkerboard tile and was completely stainless steel, cabinets and all. That was probably the most expensive thing in the entire house. They could have bought Kim at least fifty new CDs and books, James thought. But no, they had to spend it on the kitchen. The stainless steel wasn't essential to the food, now was it? No. So why did they waste all that money?

Suddenly the answer came to him, and he didn't like it: they didn't think spending money on Kim was necessary. She wasn't good enough for their money. Anger rose in him, and he coughed. One day he would show her parents just what they had in Kim.

To his left was the dining room; down the hall was the laundry room, and the bathroom to its left.

The basement was a concrete bunker. James laughed to himself. They probably had this basement put in when they built the house so they would have a place to stay in the event of a *nuclear attack*. There was a television, a couch, two recliners, matching black leather, and a bathroom. *The necessities*, he thought. *How lovely.*

He was amazed at how different the house seemed now that he was in it. He'd seen the inside of the house—well, not the basement—a million times, and now, as the walked through it, it felt completely different. He guessed he would never know why. Maybe Kim would tell him on their wedding night. His smile widened.

Then came the best part—the second floor. His heart thudded in his throat as he climbed the stairs. Directly in front of him, a few yards away, was the master bedroom. The door was closed. *Her parents don't care one bit what happens to her*, he thought. It was perfectly reasonable that a person could come into their house and take their daughter, as he would do, soon, and they *didn't care.*

He shook his head. He would always have his bedroom door open, always. Nothing would happen to Kim, he'd make sure of it. He cared about her enough to at least leave the door open.

He corrected himself—why would he have to keep his bedroom door open for Kim when Kim would be *in there with him*? He laughed, a little too loudly, caught himself, and then once he knew they were all still asleep looked around. To his right was Kim's younger brother's room. Todd was in the fifth grade, just old enough to give his sister *some* respect but young enough to annoy her till she hit him, which Kim often did. On his left was the children's bathroom. The parents had their own bathroom attached to the master bedroom. The children were not allowed to go in there, ever. Kim had once, when she was six, and her father gave her a spanking so bad she almost bled. At least that's what she told her brother a few years ago when he wanted to go in. The fear in her eyes told him she was telling the truth. James had his doubts at the time, but now he was having second thoughts. It seemed perfectly reasonable that Thomas Fehr would hit his gorgeous daughter and that Pam Watson-Fehr would let him. After all, they slept with their bedroom door closed.

He turned around, and there it was: Kim's room. He smiled and walked up to it. Her door was shut halfway: she cared enough for her little brother to pay attention to the outside. She was always watching out for him. Three nights before he had gotten sick in his bedroom, and after knocking on his parent's bedroom door for five minutes Kim came out and washed him up, changed his bed sheets, and got him to fall asleep again. Their parents never even stirred in their king-sized bed.

He stood in front of her door for the longest time. His head was spinning. So many things were taking him over: thoughts of showing Kim's parents why they should pay more attention to her; thinking maybe he should close her brother's door and do what he really wanted to do with Kim; thinking of what he would do, soon. He wanted to go in so badly it hurt, but was waiting for the right opportunity. He was waiting for his head to clear so he could soak in this moment that meant so much. This was the first time he would see her so vulnerable—up close. He hoped he would see her like this again, many times.

He opened her door. Kim was fast asleep. Only a sheet— which he knew was purple—covered her and her right leg was sticking out from under it. Her portable CD player was lying next to her, anchoring her purple and blue striped comforter to the bed. The rest of the bedclothes were piled on the floor. She was lying on her back, and James could see her flawless face perfectly. She was so beautiful he couldn't help but stare. There she was, right in front of him—his prize, his one, his only—and she was *so beautiful.* Her room was fairly empty. Along her right wall were her desk and dresser, both covered with schoolbooks and magazines. The south wall was her walk-in closet. Her left wall was one long bookshelf, overflowing with at least a hundred books, none of them school-related. Kim loved to read more than anything else. Next to it were three stacks of CDs, at least a hundred of them.

He had memorized them and her books one day a lifetime before when she was gone and he was waiting for her to come back. Back then he never followed her. He was ashamed of his former cowardice. He was so glad he bought that telescope. His binoculars were good, but he couldn't make out every little detail with them like he wanted to. The telescope gave him unlimited viewing potential. He had every inch of her room memorized. Kim's "new station" was exactly like it, order of books, CDs, and all, just it had black carpet like she wanted.

He made another mental note to put the piano he was going to buy first thing in the morning in her "new station." It would look nice in front of her walk-in closet, which wasn't really a closet at all. It was just two mirrored doors hung on the wall to look like her closet. She had many luxuries in her "new station," but he couldn't get her a walk-in closet.

She'd get over it.

He admired her for a few more minutes and then calmly walked out. As he closed the door back into its first position, he glanced back at her. She was going to make him the happiest man alive.

He coolly went down the stairs and out the front door. He locked it behind him. They'd never know he had been there.

When he walked into the house across the street, his temporary residence for the past three years, he threw out the pair of latex gloves he was wearing. His hands itched like crazy—he was allergic to latex, but there could be no evidence he had been in Kim's house. No one could know he had been there, looked at her, violated her privacy. His face widened in a grin. *Violated.* What a perfect word for this entire situation. As he undressed and slid into bed he decided that he would make his next move, the big one, three days from then.

He smiled as he slept.

* * *

The next three days were the worst of James Richardson's life. He had no idea that having to wait would be this hard, this painful. He actually *ached.* He was so excited and nervous that it was excruciating. But he waited, because *good things come to those who wait.* That was his motto, at least for now, or in any situation like this, although he highly doubted he would be in another position like this. He hoped he'd never have to do this again, God willing. After all, Kim Fehr wouldn't want to leave. But then again, his "good thing" wouldn't be coming to him, now would she? He wrote *good things have the right to be taken* on the south wall of his bedroom.

He counted the minutes.

Nothing extraordinary happened during those three days, which was good, because any added attention to Kim and her family would be dangerous for him when he executed his plan. He needed everything to be in its right place. And, luckily, everything was.

The first day was Kim's last day of school. She came home, skipped up the sidewalk, which he loved because she looked so vibrant, radiant, innocent. He laughed to himself when he realized he was going to take that innocence. The rest of the afternoon Kim, and later Todd when he got home from school, he had two weeks left before his school closed, watched TV. Kim laughed not only at the television, but at him. She was free. He was still in prison.

Her family had grilled chicken in Alfredo for dinner. That was Kim's favorite meal. Her favorite meal on her favorite day—the last day of school. Her freedom awaited her. That night she watched old episodes of *South Park* on DVD until one in the morning. Then she went to sleep, so preoccupied by thoughts of what she would do when she woke that she didn't turn off the lamp she kept on her dresser.

James took the liberty of turning it off for her at about 3, once he knew she was fast asleep. He knew she was down for the count because he had been sitting on the stairs outside her room for almost an hour.

The second day was the worst because he knew that the next day all his planning would pay off. That day was also bad, at the beginning, because Kim went to her cousin's house to watch movies and eat frozen pizza. He was glad he had tapped the

Fehrs's telephone because of moments just like that. If Kim had left and he didn't know why, he would have burst. But even though he knew where she was going, when he heard Kim's telephone conversation with Danielle and they made their plans, his heart sank. He wouldn't be able to watch her.

But James decided to work on his talents and try to make his afternoon brighter. He watched Kim, and Danielle, who was also pretty, he noted, from the laundry room of Danielle's basement. They never even suspected someone else was in the house with them. They were so happy school was over that they completely lost themselves in their euphoria. They had no idea what he could have done and what he was going to do. No one had a clue, and that made it a hundred times better.

That night Kim ate a bowl of cereal for dinner, Frosted Flakes, and listened to music in her bedroom until she fell asleep.

While she slept, James made sure he had everything he needed. He didn't sleep.

* * *

Day three began officially at nine a.m., when Kim woke up. She didn't eat breakfast, which James found a little irresponsible—after all, *breakfast is the most important meal of the day*—but he dealt with it. All that meant was that she'd need a few extra calories when he fed her that night. Kim used the time she would have spent eating to get dressed for mowing the lawns.

Kim mowed two lawns: her family's and the next door neighbor's. She mowed the family lawn because her brother was too small, her father too lazy, and her mother had to keep her nails perfect. She cut the neighbor's grass because the neighbor couldn't. Their neighbor was in her late sixties, and there was no way she could push a lawnmower, so Kim happily did it for her.

If nothing else, it was an easy ten bucks. That day she mowed the lawns like she did every Thursday. James thought that no one had ever mowed a lawn so gracefully. He marveled at the fact that everything Kim did was perfect. *God help him, he loved her so much.* He also admired the way the exercise she was getting by cutting the grass was helping her figure. He laughed to himself. *Right, Kim really needs help with her figure.* But she was losing some weight, and that upped her self-esteem, which is always good. What James wanted more than anything was for Kim to be happy. That was really all that mattered.

After all this was said and done, she would be happy. And they'd be together. Two incredibly happy people together, forever. *Finally.* It felt like he'd been waiting for Kim *forever.* It had only been three years, but it felt like an eternity. Those were, without a doubt, the longest three years of his life. But now Kim was so close to being his. She was smart, beautiful, exquisite—everything he had ever wanted. She would make him so happy.

Along with getting improved self-esteem, Kim was also getting stronger, faster: she finished chopping the grass to pieces fifteen minutes earlier than she normally did. That didn't bother James; he'd been ready for quite some time. He'd been waiting for this *exact moment* for *years.*

After mowing the lawns, Kim took a shower, like she always did. Cutting the grass always made her feel so *dirty.* Even if it didn't, she'd still take a shower because she loved them. She loved the water, loved how the heat of the water and the steam just melted away any stress she had. It was only a little after ten in the morning, sure, what stress could there be, but she couldn't deny that even thinking about showering made her feel much better.

As she turned around and stepped to the back of the shower to get her shampoo, she thought she felt a slight chill, only for a moment. When she turned around, a man she had never even seen before was standing no more than six inches in front of her. She could see the water bouncing off his back, off his dark red coat. *He was wearing a coat?* He was smiling.

She tried to scream then, but no sound came out. She tried to move, to do *anything*, but she was frozen. Finally, her mind came back to her, and she moved backward slightly.

As soon as James Richardson saw her think about moving, he lunged at her. He put a towel to her face, slightly damp, and she choked on it. She began to cough and tried to breathe in, and when she finally did it tasted like salt. Her eyes began to flutter. Everything was hazy, somewhat blue and red, and then there was only black.

* * *

Oh my good God, where am I was the first thing she thought when she woke up. Then *shit, my head hurts.* Her vision was blurry and that sent a jolt of shock through her. She blinked a thousand times and shook her head, which only made the dull throbbing she felt in her head worse. Her eyes watered furiously, and she thought she might be crying. Her throat was dry and burned. Maybe that's why her eyes were watering. There were a thousand maybes running through her head, and she became very frightened. But slowly her vision returned.

All of her fear slid off her—she was in her room.

She lay back down on her bed and started to relax. What a horrible dream that was. The last thing she remembered was taking a shower after mowing the lawns. She was washing her hair when….oh my God! There was a man! She became frantic. What happened after that? Who was he? How did I get back into my room?

She looked around and slowly realized that this was not her

room. Her room had….well, it had all the things this room did except it didn't have black carpet. Why did this room have black carpet? She got off the bed. This room was identical to hers. The CDs were in order—in alphabetical order by artist and then by release date, just like she had them at home. All of her books were there….*what the hell was going on?* All she knew for sure was that someone had taken her, and that person had put her in a room identical to hers.

There was no clock in her room so she had no idea how long she'd been there. She felt like she had been asleep for days. She slowly began to come back to reality and then in a split second she remembered what was happening. She checked the door three more times, looked the walls over again, and again, and even though she knew it was useless she still tried to find a way out.

When she was finally sure there was no way to leave, she returned to the bed and began to cry again. She had never felt so alone, unloved, abandoned. As she cried to herself she began to mumble. She did that sometimes when she was really, really upset. *Why am I here I mean I didn't do anything….it's not my fault….not my….no not really how are they gonna survive oh God I just feel so awful….why am I in this Godforsaken place I just wanna feel like….go home….*it continued like that for almost an hour.

Then, just as she was drifting off to sleep, the doorknob began to turn.

* * *

Kim had her back to the door, fearful of what she might see. She closed her eyes. She was determined not to look up. And God, it took forever for that door to open. The creaking it made as it slowly came towards her was a high-pitched squeal. Her ears rang. Her head pounded and her jaw began to ache from her clenched teeth. There was a slight scraping noise, like wood against metal that echoed in her head. She winced. She was beginning to get lightheaded—she realized she was holding her breath. She thought she might pass out. But she did not look up. There was a loud *click* as the door opened and then two clicks when the door locked. She was trapped in here with whoever took her, or whoever this was. It might not even be the person who kidnapped her, just someone who did his dirty work.

But whoever it was, she could feel him standing over her, watching, waiting for her to look back at him. She could feel his eyes burning into her. It was disgusting. She had goose bumps all over her and began to shake uncontrollably. She felt the sudden urge to vomit, but swallowed it back. She closed her eyes even tighter. She did not look up.

He put a blanket over her.

What? She had been kidnapped—surely whoever did it wanted something from her. And he wouldn't get it, whatever it was. No sir, no how. And because of that he'd probably use force. He'd hit her, hurt her, kill her. He'd torture her in unthinkable ways. He'd make her do whatever he wanted—and she'd do it, to avoid the pain, the unspeakable pain....

But whoever it was that was with her now had just put a blanket on her to keep her from shivering, so maybe he *didn't* want to hurt her. He just wanted her to be warm. He just wanted her to be comfortable, as comfortable as she could be under the circumstances.

This made no sense. Maybe it wasn't so bad after all.

Yes it was. It was terrible. This was the worst thing that had ever happened to her. And she would get herself out of this. She could think herself free, she knew she could. He couldn't beat her. She smiled to herself. Whoever did this to her didn't stand a chance. She'd start her "plan" to escape now.

She rolled over and slowly opened her eyes. Sitting directly in front of her, not two feet away, was not what she expected to see. She was startled: he didn't have three eyes, he wasn't frothing at the mouth, ready to eat her, and he didn't have anything to hurt her with (that she could see anyway). He wasn't a monster. He was quite good-looking, in fact. He was in his early twenties, with longer brown hair, and long legs. He was wearing comfortably baggy jeans and a yellow shirt unbuttoned to mid-chest. He looked muscular. He had his legs and arms crossed and he was smiling at her. That smile was disarming, comforting, like seeing a close friend at your bedside after waking from a horrible nightmare. He was always smiling at her; maybe he was in on some joke she didn't know about.

She wouldn't dare admit it out loud, but she liked him. Somehow, she liked him.

"Are you all right?" he asked. His voice was pleasant, soothing. "You were shivering, so I gave you a blanket. I thought it might help. I hope that's okay."

She didn't answer, busy with thoughts of how horrible this was but yet how much she *liked* it, the thrill of it, especially after seeing this man and how intently he was looking at her, like he really cared. He seemed genuinely concerned. But God, this was disgusting. He had *kidnapped* her. His voice, which she *really* liked now that she could focus on it, brought her out of her daze.

"Kim, my name is James Richardson and I promise I won't hurt you. I think you'll like it here more than at your own house. That's part of why I took you; just one of the many reasons." His eyes were sympathetic and concentrated; he was staring directly into her. They shimmered. He continued, "you have nothing to be afraid of, I swear." There was a long pause. "*Kim?*"

She shook her head slowly. Her throat was on fire, and she coughed every few words. "I'm, I'm sorry. I'm fine…. I think."

Her voice was raspy and she thought that made her sound weak. She tried to cough whatever it was up, or jar whatever it was down, to keep her voice calm and cool. She needed to appear in control, though there was no way she was. While she worked to adjust herself, James watched her silently and patiently. When she finally felt her throat was clear she said, "thank you for the blanket. It helped a lot."

"So you're feeling better?"

"A little."

"Good." He nodded slightly. "Think you're well enough for a little food?"

He arched his eyebrows, and it was comical. Kim didn't know if this James Richardson was doing it on purpose, though he probably was, but he was definitely charming. He was friendly and attentive. She smiled, again, but it saddened her to think that during these past three *minutes* she had smiled more than she had in the past three *months*. But still, looking at James, she smiled a little more.

Her head told her, *somehow, work your way out of this.*

"Yes, James Richardson, I think some food would be quite nice."

They both smiled, and then laughed. It came easily.

She tried to stifle the fear inside of her. All the horrible thoughts and possibilities were even more vivid now that she had seen the man who would do them to her. He stood up and swept his arm toward the door in a grand gesture.

"Let's go," he said. He bowed slightly. "I have your four-course meal for tonight already prepared. Your dining table is ready, fit for a queen—decked out with paper plates and plastic cups!" They both smiled. As they walked to the door, James's arm hovering around her waist, careful not to touch but reassuringly enough, the most terrible thought came to her. And even though she hoped it wasn't true, the thought came to her all the same: *you* belong *here.*

* * *

She was in a house, a big one. There was a small hallway, carpeted black, leading out of her room with fifteen stairs, also carpeted, at the end. There was a door at the top of the stairs. James told her to stand where she was. He went to the other side. Kim heard him lock the door. "Try it," he said.

She did, and the knob would not turn. She tried again, harder, but it was useless. As James opened the door and held it open for her, he said, "don't even think about trying to use this door, or any other door. They can only be locked and unlocked from the outside and I have the keys."

James locked the door, a bulky key ring in his hand. Kim watched carefully. All of the keys were silver; they looked identical. She wondered how he knew which key was which.

Behind them was a long wall. To their right was a hallway with two doors, both shut. To their left was a kitchen, fully furnished, with a rusty stove and decades-old refrigerator. Next to the kitchen was an open room with a television and two blue recliners. James led Kim through the kitchen into a room blocked by the wall. There was a lamp in the farthest right corner, nothing else. To their left were stairs. At the top of the stairs was another hallway. There were five doors, all shut. He took her to the second door on the right. James had to work the doorknob a bit, but once it had been jiggled sufficiently he bowed to her again as he held the door open. "Welcome to the dining room, my queen," he said.

The room was empty save the table and two chairs. The table was dark wood, sturdy, and was decorated by a rainbow-colored woven runner. The chairs matched the table, but had decorative legs and backs. There was a plate before each chair, sitting on large white napkins. The silverware was set like at a fancy restaurant, with light pink napkins underneath them. The glasses were frosted and had water in them, which gave them a strange blue glow. The meal for the night: chicken Alfredo and garlic bread, her favorite.

As they ate they seldom talked, only chatting about how she was feeling and James insisting that she would like it here and that she had nothing to fear. Unfortunately, Kim felt he was right and began to settle in, however uncomfortable it remained. *You belong here.*

* * *

Once they were finished eating, James led her back to her room. As they walked she noticed he was extremely skinny. His clothes clung to him and she thought she saw the outline of his ribs. He also walked with a slight limp. She wondered what had happened to him. Had he gotten hurt? Was he born like that?

It made her a little uncomfortable to be wondering about him. She didn't need to be thinking about it, to be concerned about his life or well-being. A part of her was still wary, telling her to find a way out, to do whatever it took to get free. Another part began to get comfortable.

He opened the door to her room, opening his hand to usher her in. He said goodnight to her, sharply, bowed his head, and left. She tried to say goodnight, to talk to him, but he left too quickly. She put her ear to the door; she could hear him walking away, his keys jangling quietly. She cried herself to sleep, for many very different reasons.

* * *

At about 5 pm on the night of her disappearance, Kim's parents came home to find their daughter gone. She hadn't left a note, which was unlike her, and that made them worry. They called all her friends and some local relatives, but no one had seen her. They called the police, who after the standard twenty-four hour mark finally considered her missing and half-heartedly investigated. There were no leads, which proved intriguing, especially since Kim had not been the type to just run away, but they marked her up as a runaway just as well and her case was forgotten. Kim's parents hired a private investigator, which turned up nothing, but they kept trying. After six months, their hopes began to dwindle and they contemplated burying her.

They should have.

* * *

The first two weeks were the hardest. Kim passed the time in her room looking for a way out, some kind of fault in the walls she could use, but there was nothing. By the third day she had established James' schedule. He would wake very early, shower, and dress. She could hear him moving around above her. Then there would be quiet. After about an hour or so, she didn't know exactly because she didn't have a clock, he would come down and let her come upstairs for a shower.

She had fifteen minutes to shower and dress; if she went past her allowance he would come in and turn the water off for her. The first day he had nearly done it, but she screamed when he opened the door, and swung at him when he tried to open the shower curtain. After that she was finished long before he would need to come in. Although at times she wished he would, so she

PREDILECTION

could drown him. Then he would take her into the dining room
for breakfast and after that into her room. Sometimes they would
talk, sometimes not. The routine was basically the same for lunch
and dinner. Sometimes he would bring her dessert downstairs, or
breakfast in bed. She had a remote that would page him whenever
she needed to use the restroom. On good days he would stay with
her and they would talk, just small talk; on bad days he would push
her into the room once he opened the door and slam it in her face.

She learned very quickly that you did not want to cross him on
bad days.

One morning, lost in thought, she went over her fifteen
minutes in the shower and James burst in. Before she could
protest he had flung the shower curtain open, knocked her
backwards, hitting her head against the tile, and turned off the
water. She fell hard on her tailbone. He bent down, slapped her
across the face as hard as he could. She curled up and cried after
a moment's shock. James looked at her curiously as she cried,
covering herself, and then he walked out. Her cheek burned.
"You have five minutes to get dressed and get out here," he said
sternly. She did it in two.

When she emerged from the bathroom, still crying, James
grabbed her by the arm and half-drug her to her room. He pushed
her into the room and went to slam the door but her ankle was in
the way. The force of the door bent it sideways and she screamed
in pain. He looked down, indifferently, and kicked her foot out of
the way. He slammed the door so hard it shook the floor. She
heard him stomp up the stairs. Her ankle and tailbone hurt so
badly she could barely walk, or sit, or stand. Maybe she had
broken them. She was confused and shocked and began to cry
again. As she lay curled on her bed, trying to stop her tears, he
stormed in. She turned to face him, started to apologize, but he
told her to shut up and roll over. She cried harder, feeling nausea

rise, but then he was on top of her, his knee digging into her back. She let out a small yelp of pain, but he didn't stop; he grabbed her arms, twisted them backward, and tied her wrists together. He stuffed a handkerchief into her mouth and knotted it where her neck met her head. Then he tied her ankles and rolled her onto her back. She squirmed around and screamed through her tears, begging him to stop, but the wild anger in his eyes made her break off. She knew he would never stop.

"I'm sorry; I don't want to do this, but I have to," he whispered softly in her ear as he slid off the bed.

She could not see it, nor did she feel it as the wretchedness of what was happening overwhelmed her, but his tears fell silently on her shoulders. She began to weep even louder, her sobs thundering up from deep inside of her. She began to beg, unintelligibly. *Please stop.*

He picked up a strange orange box. He ripped off her gag and placed the large, metal-hinged box made out of plywood over her head. It was heavy; the neck hole choked her. The interior was carpeted. It was very hard to breathe. She realized that she could not hear, talk, or see.

He left her like that for five days, letting her out of the box once a day for food and letting her give herself a sponge bath. He watched her while she bathed, and she couldn't be sure, but she thought he had been with her the whole time, just watching her.

The darkness was suffocating at first. It enveloped all her senses—the tickling push of the carpet against her skin, the sticky wet at the center of her face from her tears, snot, and spit; the faint musk smell of the carpet, the heaviness of her eyelids from straining to hold them open. Her throat was raw from all her useless screaming and begging, her chest weighted from the tremendous effort it took to breathe—all of it was nothing compared to the darkness. She had never been bothered by darkness before. She had been somewhat fond of it, in fact; she had always found herself more creative at night, but this was completely different. The darkness crept into her mind through her mouth, ears. It came through her eyes and blended with her tears; it slithered down her throat, wrapped itself around her, and smothered her. It took up residence inside her and slid its cold fingers down her spine. She completely gave into it. She let it devour her, and was surprised to find herself already within it. The darkness fused within her and she knew what she had to do.

Whenever James would take the box off of her, once she refocused her eyes she saw him smiling. It was quite a pleasant smile, actually. She thought about James a lot of the time she was in the darkness, and discovered that he was distinctly appealing. Then he would feed her, tell her that this was for her own good, and then replaced the box, the wet, thick mat of the carpet sliding down her face.

At first she hated the darkness, and the fear it brought that consumed her, but by the time James brought her back to the light for good, she did not want to go.

* * *

"You broke your promise," was the first thing she said to him after he had taken the box off of her ("for good, I hope," he had said) and she had showered and dressed. She didn't know how long she had been in the box, but it had seemed like weeks. While she was in the darkness, when not reveling in it, she thought. She thought about her family, this situation she was in—and if/how she should get out of it—and James; when she thought of James her heart began to beat a little faster, but she was still slightly wary of him and a little disgusted. But he had helped her, given her food, kept her safe, and with no way out she felt she needed him.

But he had also promised he would not hurt her, when they first met, when she woke up in this strange room. By the look on his face, she could tell he didn't know what she was talking about; he didn't remember.

"When your first brought me here, you said, 'Kim, my name is James Richardson and I promise I won't hurt you.' That's what you said. What do you call sticking me in that thing?" She looked at the box, sitting next to the doorway, and started to weep. Her neck had a long rug burn on it from the carpet of the box. Her neck was sore, but it also felt absent, like it wasn't even there. She was operating in the back of her mind.

He was looking at her with slightly mocking eyes.

"Yes, I did say that," he spoke slowly, calmly, "but I also told you that there were rules you had to follow. And you agreed to accept the consequences if you broke those rules."

Kim thought for a moment. Yes, he had said that, and she had agreed. She had no reply. James narrowed his eyes.

"If you break the rules again, I have a much bigger box you can stay in." She realized he meant a coffin, her death, and as her eyes widened with recognition, he raised his eyebrows questioningly, to warn her not to challenge his authority and take what he had said without defiance; then he smiled. The smile was warm; it completely brightened his face.

He laughed.

"It's not like that," he said. "But I could do that if I wanted to."

* * *

The next few weeks were uneventful. Kim had learned that it was best to follow directions, and she did whatever James asked, no question. He never asked anything extraordinary or inappropriate, which may or may not have made a difference.

Kim wasn't sure if she would refuse him, no matter what he asked, just because he could put her in that box again. It wasn't the darkness of the box that frightened her, she had embraced the darkness, she actually liked it now; but the carpet of the box she detested. The thick, wet matting against her face, the way it hindered her breathing. That she could not stand. The darkness was no longer a concern; she had begun to sleep with the covers over her face, to stay in the black. It was actually calming. But James had also threatened her with a sleeping box, which confused her. She didn't know exactly what he meant, but she did not really wish to know.

James was not sure if he should give Kim any more liberties, but it hadn't been that long since he punished her. He felt bad about it, but he'd had to. The box was a horrific thing; he had worn it when it was still being built, and it was terrifying. It had torn him apart, actually made him weep, to hear her scream at the top of her lungs and see her wrenching on the floor. He had had to sleep in a room on the second floor instead of his usual room a few doors down from Kim. The noise of her suffering was unbearable; he had to get away from it. He decided to keep things the way they were for a few more days, maybe a week. Then they could move forward.

It was nearly three weeks before Kim would disobey again. They had been getting along extremely well, becoming quite close. It took a while, but soon Kim found she trusted James enough to tell him things she had never told anyone else. James opened up easily once Kim did. They shared stories from their childhoods, good and bad, made jokes, shared some secrets. They were quite fond of each other.

But then Kim got upset at something James said, and they

began to argue. James grabbed her by her arms and drug her to his room. He threw her onto the bed and she curled up, screaming and weeping. Whenever James became violent like that, suddenly, she would become nearly hysterical. There was no apparent reason for it—she did not need to react as strongly as she did. But James could retaliate equally.

He yelled at Kim to stay on the bed, and he threw back the covers. She began to scream again, fearful he would try to violate her. He didn't—instead he grabbed a hold of something under the bed and pulled it out with a grunt. He leapt over it and onto the bed, grabbing Kim and pulling her off the bed, holding her arms behind her back to block her thrashing. She was out of control. She was screaming at the top of her lungs, kicking him, even trying to bite him. He threw her to the ground, straddled her, and slapped her across the face as hard as he could. She froze, agape, which was what he had wanted. He stepped away from her, and once she quieted, although she was still sniffling and her breath was catching, he picked her back up. "This is what you will get if you keep this attitude," he said.

It was a simple plywood box that fit perfectly under his bed. It was actually two boxes, one bigger than the other. He stood her up next to it and ordered her to lie down inside the smaller box. She shook her head no; he told her he would cut out her tongue if she didn't get in. She crawled in. He made her roll over onto her back; she had to get half-way out of the box to do it, it was so small. Once she had, he pushed the box under the bed. She could not see or move. It was like she was in a coffin. It was unbearable. She could not move her arms or legs to hit or kick, so she screamed as loud as she could. She had to get out of that thing. She screamed, and she screamed. Gasping for air, she tried to move her head, to move anything, but she could not, so she opened her eyes wide to try to see *anything* and opened her mouth so wide her jaw hurt. She screamed. And she screamed.

"You will do as I say or I will keep you in this until you rot alive," he said calmly. She did not hear him, but she knew what he had said, she knew it was a warning. There was always a warning; you had to give him that.

Then there was a slight shaking and light flooded around her. James had pulled it back out.

Kim clawed and climbed her way out of the box, coughing and crying on her knees. James repeated himself to make sure she had heard him. Kim was so scared she just nodded her head without any real sense of why. She had never been so frightened in her life. Then James thrust the box back under the bed, covered it with the sheets, and knelt beside her. He wrapped his arms around her and she buried her face in his chest, weeping like a child. He whispered to her that everything was going to be fine, as long as she followed the rules, and she choked out sobs that were supposed to agree with him. She could not speak. James carried her to her room and laid her on the bed. She fell asleep quickly and stayed asleep for a long, long time. It was so much more peaceful when she was asleep. She liked the comfort in the darkness, the black that wrapped its arms around her and held her close.

She awoke in the middle of the night, her head throbbing and her nose stuffy after the tears. She thought of James above her, in his room in the small house. She accepted she would never leave.

His moods seemed to be consistent, but then the pattern would break and she could no longer gauge him anymore. Those were the worst times: when she had no idea what he was thinking. Because he could be thinking of a movie he saw, or the weather that day, or how badly he wanted to break her nose. She could never know for sure in those moments, and they frightened her worse than she could describe. Most of the time she assumed he wanted to break her.

* * *

It is a strange thing when violence causes dependency and love instead of hate. The fear of violence may bring about strange feelings and doings, but violence can also birth a certain trust. The trust that if you do as you are told, are good, then you will be safe. It is a simple deeds-rewards-punishments system, the kind that children learn from near-infancy. If the fear is strong enough, any other feelings can be forgotten and the fear can take complete control. It's like wiping the slate clean. After that, you can start over and instill what you desire in the person, further reinforcing it with the fear of punishment. It's a fairly simple trick; it works too well.

There is also the paradox of loving a person who harms you. It is a common story: the cycle of violence is an insidious device. You walk on eggshells around the person, paralyzed because you never know what will throw him into a frenzy; he believes you deserve to be hit and so he does it; he tells you he didn't mean it and it won't happen again. And you accept it, but still tiptoe around him…until he hits you again.

There are feelings of inadequacy on both fronts; people begin to feel they deserved to be beaten or deserved to do the beating. They crawl back to each other for the acceptance because of the "if:" *If you are good, you will not get hurt again.* But you will get hurt again, and violence is catching.

* * *

Kim could no longer differentiate between her old life and the home she was now confined to. She became used to the routines, the disorganization in her own mind; she became completely indifferent to anything she came into contact with. James noticed this transition. He had not expected this turn in her and was disheartened by it. He had control over her—she always did what she was told—but there was no life in her. He wanted her to respond to him, to give attention back. He expected it. He had expected her to fall in love with him.

At first he tried to make her laugh, or just smile; he told jokes, gave her chores to do, and generally let her do things out of her normal confines. Nothing worked. She was listless, dull. It had saddened him in the beginning of his attempts because he knew how vibrant she could be, but the longer and harder his effort without result the angrier he became.

He decided to beat it out of her.

The decision came to him late one night while he lay awake trying to fall asleep. His mind was spinning, full of jumbled thoughts and memories. He was mostly thinking of the dinner they had just had—Kim sat silently at her seat, head bowed, slowly eating her Chinese food without even the slightest glance toward him or any indication of feeling. He tried to make small talk, like he always did, tried desperately to get her to come back into her old self. But nothing worked. She just sat there, mechanically taking her fork from plate to mouth, mouth to plate. She didn't even stop to take a drink. Once she put her fork down he knew she was finished for the night and he resignedly scooted his chair back and lead her to her room. He asked her if she wanted any dessert, if she would like to get a book to read from his "library" or watch some television, but she just looked at the floor or ahead of her blankly, in silence. He left the door to her room open, telling her she was welcome to come and sit with him if she wanted. Within ten minutes her light was out and ten minutes after that when he checked in on her she appeared to be sleeping. It was only 6.30. She had been sleeping a lot more lately.

He knew she would not get back up, would not come to him, and dejected, he showered and went to bed shortly after that. As he laid there, mind racing, trying to think of a way to get her to even just speak to him, his anger rose. How dare she ignore him? Wasn't he giving her everything she could need? Wasn't he going above and beyond the privileges she should be given? That ungrateful little bitch; the least she could do was say thank you. He didn't have to give her food, or possessions, or let her leave her room. He could have just locked her in that room, bare floor, no light, no nothing, and kept her in there. No shower, no food, no companionship—maybe that was what she deserved. Here he was, giving her the best he had, because he loved her so much, and she wouldn't even look at him.

If she won't say thank you on her own, he thought, then I'll just make her say it.

As he walked toward her room, he realized he was slowing down, becoming more cautious as each step drew him closer to her. Somewhere in the back of his mind he second-guessed himself, but his determination was so cold it quickly passed. He opened her door the rest of the way noiselessly. He wanted to give her an exit, let her get away, so he could hunt her down.

She was laying on her bed, under a mountain of covers, her back to him, sleeping soundly. She did not stir when he entered or as he walked closer. He slowly balled his fists, his face hardening. He stared at her for the longest time, breathing in the moment. She was so beautiful, her hair in her face, her cheekbones high. Her breathing was deep and long; his heartbeat began to pulse in the same rhythm, and when he began punching her beautiful face, arms, back, whatever his fists made contact with, his punches were in time as well.

He was on her before even he realized it, like the immediacy of a spark in the night. At first all she knew was the pain. There was one quick blow, to her shoulder, sharp pain that spread into her neck and down her arm; it numbed her fingers. She raised her opposite hand to her shoulder and leaned forward onto her thighs. Her eyes were squinted shut from the pain but she did not need to see; she knew what was happening and by whom. She knew it in the back of her mind, dimly somewhere outside the pain, the way you can feel when someone is looking at you. As she put pressure onto her shoulder, there was another bolt of pain, coming from her middle.

When she rolled onto her side she could tell it was coming from the small of her back, her kidneys. He pushed her backward, her head slamming against the headboard. He cursed at her, awful words her mind dared not acknowledge because they would have shattered her then and there. She could feel the cold wet of his spit on her face as he screamed at her, and it was in that moment that she began to beg for him to stop. But there were no words, only a jumble of syllables and moans. His words had turned into an incomprehensible rant. When she finally looked at him he stopped.

He looked at her with a strange mix of disdain and pity. Her eyes were wild with fear, her body crumpled on the bed and already turning colors, but he was too thrilled to be sorry for what he had done. So he moved away from her, slowly, took a deep breath, and hit her in the face as hard as he could. The force knocked her off of the bed to a hard landing on the floor, her head bouncing off the concrete thinly covered by carpet. There was a moment's respite, a slight peace, while James, lost in rage, did not realize she was gone. He punched the sheets and pillows, blows meant for no one but himself. After that came the labored sound of his breathing, panting, like he was coming down from climax, and then there was only silence.

From his spot on the bed, doubled over with his head in his hands, James's mind finally stopped spinning and he heard her crying for the first time. It was a deep, low sobbing, coming from her lungs. He listened as she coughed and gagged. He listened to his own thoughts, his immediate regret, and did not notice her sobs slowly stop. He was lost in black, the universe whirl pooling before him, when his unprovoked vengeance sliced itself down the back of his calf.

He involuntarily grabbed at the pain, feeling hot blood on his fingers, and let out a sound Kim had never heard before; it made her hesitate. She had not expected it: he sounded like a dog, a deep, guttural yawp. He looked up at her, saw his pocketknife in her hands. The knife must have fallen out of his pocket when he jumped onto the bed; now she was armed. Bewildered, he tried to calm her.

"Kim, I—"

He got no further.

Her eyes narrowed, her lips pursed, and she went to him, resolute. She pushed him backward and stabbed the knife into his shin as hard as she could. He screamed and grabbed at her hands, but she was pushing him away with one hand and pushing the knife in slowly with the other. Then, she twisted the knife, feeling it grind against bone.

The pain was excruciating. It went through his entire leg, as if there was not one particular source, and traveled up the left side of his body, making him feel strangely numb despite the agony. There was blood everywhere. It gushed onto the bed, a sticky current that ran down the covers onto the floor, soaking into the carpet. James's leg looked suspended from his body, twisted at a disjointed angle, the knee high into the air, foot hanging limply. He lay heavily on the bed, arms sprawled but bent at his sides. His head hung away from the pain, his breathing hurried and shallow, tears glistening on his cheeks, sighing a mush of pain and exhaustion.

Kim had enjoyed it than she thought she would. Her initial reaction, once her adrenaline took over and she heard him thrashing the bed, was that she had nothing else to do but defend herself. She had only moments, she knew; the knife was only a foot away from her, the metal edging of its case glinting off the hallway light. She stretched for it, her arm feeling like it was pulled so tightly it would snap. She could not reach it. She crawled forward, on her elbows, pushed against the floor, and grabbed the knife. She fumbled with the casing, her hands slick from sweat and blood, unable to pull the knife out. She wiped her hands on her shirt hurriedly, and then, with newfound resilience, extracted the blade. It was long, and sharp.

She stood up; saw him doubled over on the bed. His right leg was outstretched, his jeans pulled up, exposing the calf. Without thinking, she sliced the knife down the middle, one quick, sleek cut, and when she heard him gasp and react with instant reflexes, she jumped back, knife held out toward him. She had expected him to fight, but he did nothing but hold the leg, stuttering at her. He looked incredibly vulnerable. She liked it.

When the knife drove into his shin, stopping against the bone, she could have made a run for the door. She could have found the way out—there was no way he could get to her in time. But she did not try to escape. Instead, she watched the way his face changed and contorted, listened to the sounds he was making—sparking in her mind sexual flashes—and saw she did not like, but *loved* it.

When she stuck the knife into his shin she had done so out of defense, although not reflexively, perhaps there was some spite in her. But when she put one hand on his thigh and twisted the knife with the other, she did it because she wanted to; the power she had over him, the look on his face, was lascivious.

At that moment, like a snap of a twig, her mind shifted and she saw what he had been doing, why, and how he felt. She understood him.

She watched him writhe in pain a little longer, pushing herself against the fabric of her pants, enjoying the friction, and then went to him. She put her arms around him and helped him off the bed.

"We have to get this taken care of or you'll never walk on this leg again," she said.

James looked at her with confused eyes and, after a moment, nodded. So now they knew each other. They could be together, as he had wanted: completely. He hung onto her shoulders, pushed his legs closer together, and working together they half-drug him upstairs, trying not to leave too big a trail of blood, and got him into the car. Kim drove them to the emergency room. It was the first time she had driven a car in just less than a year, and she was happy.

The Four Stages
of Destruction

Conception

It began on a beautiful early fall day in Illinois, the kind of day one is happy to be alive. The leaves had just begun to turn but there was still vibrancy to all the greenery that remained; the sun beamed down undauntedly. Its rays were welcoming rather than overwhelming. It was the perfect kind of day for an ice cream.

Barnesville, a small college town, had just opened a major, although fashionable, ice cream franchise in its new downtown add-on. The place was spacious and bright; there were twelve different flavors and a plethora of additional toppings you could mix into your treat. It made more money than anyone could have hoped.

When Kathryn Harper walked into Ice Cold all she could think of was the Triple-Chocolate-and-Brownie Delight. She had been having a bad week; but her classes had been canceled for the day, there had been fewer children at the day care where she worked, and fall, her favorite season, had officially begun after three unbelievably hot October days. Indian Summer was over, taking with it the humidity that had suffocated the summer. Things were looking up, and this ice cream would be a welcome start to her weekend—except for the long line. "The Cold," as her college peers called it, was always crowded, but it was particularly packed that night. She hated crowds and waiting in line, but this ice cream would be worth it. Nothing could break her good mood.

It was at this moment, as it usually happens, when her elated spirit put her guard down, that he appeared.

She noticed him only because she heard the bell of the door. Otherwise, she wouldn't have turned around. But she did, and when she saw him it was like walking straight into a wall. He was in his late twenties, thirty at the most, tall, and lean, not too skinny, unshaven, with brown hair that was on the longer side. His stubble of a beard and hair would have made him look sloppy, but his jeans were fitted, his red polo shirt clean and pressed. He seemed to have an athletic build, and as he quickly smiled at her, he brushed his hair from his eyes. He had long, slender fingers. No ring. She smiled back.

It happened in mere seconds, with one glance, but in that moment she felt the slightest hope of love.

Her face suddenly felt hot. She turned around to hide the red in her cheeks. What was going on? She never felt like this. She had checked out plenty of men, from afar, but this time it was different—perhaps because she got caught? Or was it because he looked back? As the line moved forward she could feel his eyes on her. Usually she hated the feeling of people looking at her, but this time it was vaguely enjoyable. It seemed it took forever for her turn to be waited on. He had to be staring at her. She turned and pretended to look around the place. He was definitely looking at her.

She wondered why that suddenly mattered to her. She was a sadly pretty girl, in a homely way, average height with some meat on her bones. She wasn't fat, but she wasn't skinny. Some of her friends described her *chunky*, but that wasn't quite right either. She was boringly normal. Occasionally she would catch guys giving her the once-over, but she thought nothing of it. Maybe that was it—no one had ever stared at her like he was staring. No one had ever looked at her in a way that made her *feel*, as his eyes did. Maybe she *wanted* him to stare. It didn't hurt that he was pretty good looking himself.

When only one person stood between her and her ice cream, she glanced around again. This time their eyes met and lingered. Something passed between them, something like recognition, and then he broke away. He looked over her shoulder.

"Miss, what can I get for you today?"

His number, she thought.

She got her Triple-Chocolate-Delight, in a smaller size than she had planned; she didn't want to seem like a fatso if he heard her order. He got something that resembled a banana split, with extra chocolate chips. She smiled to herself as she watched him, in short glimpses, while their orders were made. He was quite attractive. Every time she looked at him she caught him returning the look, and then they both looked at the floor. She thought she saw him blush. Then they both had their treats, and turned around to wait to pay. He stood much closer to her than he had before. She could feel the heat coming off him. For a brief moment she entertained the thought of taking him into the bathroom and having her way with him, and then she thought of him naked, spread eagle on her bed, and she would lick the ice cream off him.

Embarrassed by her thoughts, she paid and hurried out the door, taking a seat outside on the patio furniture. She took her spot so she could watch him as he paid more than because she wanted to eat outside. She had actually planned to eat alone, in her SUV, listening to the radio. But her plan was thwarted: he was out the door right behind her, and when she turned to look inside he had to stop short, they were too close. His ice cream went straight into her chest. The force of their meeting made them fall into one of the flimsy metal tables, and she had to steady herself with her hips. He jumped back when he realized he was on top of her.

"I'm so sorry," he said quickly, "so sorry. Here, let me get you something to clean yourself with."

He ran into the building and grabbed some napkins before she could realize what had happened. It was the cold on her chest that finally did it. All she had known was his weight on her and falling, but the circle of cold smack in the middle of her burning chest brought her back.

"Shit," she muttered. She suddenly remembered she had an ice cream too. Where was it?—Splattered on the concrete.

"Double shit," she said, a little louder.

"Pardon?" a voice said. She turned around, startled; he handed her the napkins. "I'm so sorry," he repeated.

His voice had a slight accent, possibly British; he was staring at the stain on her chests. Kathryn felt herself flush again. He was looking at her breasts.

He said, "I was just trying to get your attention. 'Double shit'—I guess it worked." The laughter came easily, and it went on for quite a while. "Let me make it up to you," he finally said, "I'll go get you another."

"No, it's fine, really," she replied. "Don't worry about it."

"I insist."

She hesitated—why? She usually deflected such kindness.

"OK. I had a—"

"A Triple-Chocolate-Delight, right?" She looked at him with raised eyebrows. He blushed suddenly as he realized he had not looked her in the eyes, and, embarrassed, skipped a step and looked from her chest to the ground.

"I, uh, I noticed what you ordered," he said quickly, "because it sounded really good. I thought I might get the same thing."

"Oh, um, yeah, a Triple-Chocolate," she half-sighed. It was hard to talk.

"A small?" he asked.

"Yes." She sat down in one of the hard, metal folding chairs. He smiled, studied her for a moment, and then went back inside. While they made his new order he kept looking back at her, smiling. She tried to look aloof at first, paying attention to cleaning herself, but the time to play hard to get was long gone so she smiled back at him. His grin widened.

When he returned, two very large ice creams in his hands, he pointedly sat them down before he took his seat.

"Better safe than sorry," he quipped. They laughed again. "My name is Duncan."

"I'm Kathryn."

"Pleased to make your acquaintance, Kathryn," he said and shook her hand.

She giggled and immediately regretted it. Her cheeks turned another shade of red.

"As I was saying earlier," he went on, smirking at her response, "was that before I made your shirt my personal trash can, I was trying to get your attention. I was going to ask you if you'd like to go to dinner with me tomorrow night."

She was speechless. And a little confused. Had she, the great Queen Virgin, really just been asked out on a date? He waited for her to talk, but seeing her look turn from surprise to confusion, began to say something else.

She cut him off before the moment was gone: "Yes. I'd love to."

Kathryn was stunned. Nothing like this had ever happened to her before. She only been on a handful of dates, but she had known those guys for more than five minutes. But now she had agreed. No thinking left to do. Oh, what the hell; take a chance for once, her mind said. It felt right.

"Great!" he said, and grinned. She realized he had lines at the corners of his eyes. Maybe he was older than she'd thought.

They made small talk about their lives. He was a graphic designer at a local marketing agency who lived a few minutes from campus.

"That's perfect," she said, "I live near campus, in the Greenmount Apartments."

"Really? I lived in Prairie Hall," he said. "But that was a while ago." They talked about professors they had both had. Then the conversation died down and they finished in silence.

"I guess I'll see you tomorrow," she said as they threw away their trash.

"Yes," he said, taking her hand and kissing it. "I'll pick you up outside your building around seven."

* * *

It took her nearly two hours to get ready. She was never really concerned with her appearance; as long as she looked presentable that was all she needed. Even on the dates she had gone on, though there were a precious few, she had never dressed up. She had worn flattering jeans and her favorite shirts, comfortable but cute shoes. This time, she knew it was different. She had to be knockdown gorgeous; she had to make a great impression. In the end, after nearly twelve different dresses, pant, blouse, skirt, and heel combinations and three calls to various family members, she decided on her V-necked, cap sleeved black dress with her black and white polka dot belt, and heeled strapped sandals. She wore her hair down with an ornate butterfly clip. She did her make-up for the first time in nearly a year and even tried to put in her long-abandoned contact lenses; her glasses would do.

During the entire outfit ordeal she could think of nothing but Duncan, his beautiful smile, and revel in the electricity that shuddered through her whenever she pictured his face.

During their brief ice cream engagement the day before she had felt so light when she was with him—like whatever weight that had been bothering her was momentarily lifted. She felt so *happy* around him. It had been a long time since she had truly felt happy, and it was always a long time coming once it arrived and gone too soon; somehow, Duncan—a beautiful name, she thought—could pull that feeling from her with ease. And it didn't leave. Just the mere thought of him made her *ecstatic*. Accordingly, she did almost nothing but think of him the entire day. She was anxious but incredibly excited. Something was happening here, she was sure of it.

It was like the shadowed path she had been on suddenly shifted and she could plainly see the once bare trees blossoming and sunlight pouring in.

* * *

Duncan was five minutes early, which pleased Kathryn to no end. She was always punctual, sometimes horrendously early; there was nothing that she hated more than lateness. It pleased her to no end that he was not only on time, but early. She added another plus to his already long list of good characteristics. He pulled his black mustang in front her apartment complex, waved to her, parked, and got out. He had a large bouquet of flowers, red roses. He came to her in long strides and smiled.

"Hello," she said, with as much poise as she could muster— she was feeling exceptionally nervous.

He greeted her back and nearly sighed, "You look great," as he escorted her to the car, his hand near her waist but never actually touching it. They exchanged simple pleasantries.

He opened the door for her, and she laughed, "I'm not royalty, you know."

He smiled, "Yes, but a beautiful lady ought to be treated like one," and shut the door with a slight thud. He hurried around the car and slid into the black leather seat with subtle grace, like a cat, she noticed.

They made small talk on the way to the restaurant. It turned out Duncan was in advertising, his major clients including several local chain grocery and bank chains, several restaurants, including Ice Cold, two international companies, and one small record label. In college he changed his major more times than he could remember, and finally settled on Business and Marketing. He received his Master's in a year and a half. The Italian place he was taking her to had been his first client; he was still their main man.

"Remember those ads they had this summer with the crazy chef?" He asked. She nodded.

"When I first got the idea, I hated it. But my deadline was the next morning and I had nothing else. So I gave them the idea, and they went nuts. Made quite a few of them. I'm still not sure they're very good."

Kathryn thought for a moment. They were decent commercials, although the first time you saw them they were confusing as hell. The chef was making some kind of food, yelling at his staff in Italian, and then a waiter comes from behind him and pushes a large red button on his back. The chef slumps over, shakes his head, and then speaks to the audience in a normal voice. The staff calms down, and the food is finally presented. The restaurant's tagline was "good Italian food, no fuss."

She took in his intent look for a moment, and said, "I like them. A lot." He looked at her and raised his eyebrows.

"I mean it," she protested, "the first time you see that chef slump over and you think he's a robot or something, it really gets your attention." That part was not a lie; it was a good hook. But she didn't actually like them all that much. It felt strange lying to him. But he looked back at the road, satisfied. She loved that she had given him that contented look, and vowed to herself that she would do whatever it took to make sure he stayed content.

They arrived at the restaurant, a small, cozy, dimly-lit brick building that had been a Barnesville staple for three generations, about ten minutes later. It was unusually empty, especially for a Saturday night. The maitre-de greeted them eagerly, talking with Duncan about how long it had been since he'd come to the restaurant and how good he was looking. He replied politely but nothing more.

"Your usual table," he announced, "is ready for you."

The "usual table" was a two-seater in the far-left corner, nestled between a long row of other tables to its left and the divider between the smoking/non-smoking sections (which doubled as the beverage deck) on its right. There were few lights in the dark brick restaurant anyway, but it was even darker here. There were three red candles in the middle of the table and a bottle of champagne on ice standing next to the table.

The maitre-de smiled as he put the menus on the table and slowly backed away from the table, saying, "You're always welcome here, Mr. Beirstein; please come again."

Duncan slipped him some money.

"Always a pleasure, Sam," he replied.

Duncan hurried over to the table and pulled out her chair for her.

"Thank you," she said, a little shocked—such a gentleman! Soft classical music played from some hidden speaker. The candles were on an antique candelabra; the wax dripped onto a small pewter plate beneath it. Kathryn noticed that the flames were not very hot or very tall. It was as if everything about the night had been planned out to be perfect.

They each ordered, and in the candlelight Kathryn could see the few fine lines on Duncan's face, although they were softened: mostly laugh lines around his eyes, but his forehead wrinkled a little more than it should have whenever he shifted his eyebrows. She was about to ask him his age, but as soon as the thought entered her mind he offered her the champagne.

"No thanks," she said, slowly shaking her head, "I'm not old enough to drink."

"You're not?"

"No. I'm only twenty. I'll be twenty-one in a few months."

"Wow. I thought you were at least twenty-five." He grew silent, looking like he was suddenly deep in thought.

Kathryn was worried. People had always thought she was older than she actually was, had since she was sixteen, but no one ever seemed bothered when she told them otherwise. Seeing Duncan concentrating on something far away made her nervous. She liked him so much; she hoped her age wasn't a deal breaker.

"I get that all the time," she said hastily.

"I…I can see why," he said slowly. "Wow. Oh well. It makes no difference."

"Are you sure?" She had to know he was going to stay.

"Yes, I'm sure." He smiled slowly. "You could have some champagne if you wanted; I promise I won't tell," he teased.

Kathryn smiled—what a relief. The playful look he had made him look much younger. She thought for a moment as he looked at her with a slightly devilish grin.

"I guess one glass won't hurt," she finally said.

"Now we're talking," he said, taking her long-stemmed glass and pouring it full of a sparkling, pale cream liquid. It smelt quite good. She took a sip; it tasted good as well. She wondered what he tasted like.

"Mmm," she said, "it's very good."

"I'm glad you like it," Duncan smiled. He looked so much older than she thought he was. Kathryn couldn't take it anymore.

"You know all about me," she said, "so how old are you?" She gave him a little wink and smirked.

"Why do you ask? Does it matter?" He was playful again—it was remarkable how chameleon-like his facial expressions could be, how fluently they changed.

"I only ask because this dim light is making me have to focus on you very hard, and those lines by your eyes speak volumes to me."

"What?! The botox is failing?" They both laughed. "If you must know, I'm thirty-six."

"Huh." She was silent for a long moment. He was sixteen years her senior.

"Does that bother you?"

"Not at all."

"Good."

Their meal arrived. They talked about anything and everything; they finally left the restaurant two hours later. He took her back to her apartment, opening the door for her to get out like a valet. They stood together for a minute.

She was about to ask him up when he asked, "Let's do this again?"

"Please. As soon as possible."

"I'll give you a call—tomorrow," he said with an intent tone.

"That'd be great."

"OK. Tomorrow it is. Talk to you later!" He gave her a quick kiss on the cheek and darted into his car. He waved to her as he drove away. Sleek like a cat, she thought as she watched him drive away. His movements were sharp and long.

She had very sweet dreams that night.

Maintenance

For the next two months they talked to each other on the phone every day. They had fun, easy conversations, lots of laughs, but they covered semi-serious ground as well, like children and marriage (in general), and some basics about politics and religion. Kathryn tried to avoid the latter subjects because they tended to evoke strong feelings, and she didn't like confrontation nor did she have strong feelings herself. It was a wonderful time. Various schedule conflicts kept them from going out more than twice a week, but when they managed it was incredible.

On their third date they had their first kiss. They had gone out to see a scary movie, an intelligent one, they were both relieved to see. So many were simple blood and gore movies, but theirs had a shock and a depth that they agreed they hadn't seen in a movie for a long time. They were both happy that their taste in movies and music meshed. They had gone to get a drink (he coffee, her strawberry lemonade) afterwards to talk about the film. Duncan took her home about an hour later; when they talked, they talked for a long time. There was so much they agreed on, but their differences were big enough to warrant elaboration. Duncan loved Kathryn's intellect most of all—he still had a hard time believing she was so much younger than he.

Once they arrived at her apartment building, Kathryn got up the nerves to ask him up. He readily agreed. Once they got to her studio apartment, just big enough for a small futon, desk, small TV/VCR, and a large bookshelf, they both became tense. They sat on her futon for a few minutes, a local rock station humming in the background.

"So, I—"

"Do you think—" they said simultaneously.

They both began to laugh, and before Kathryn had stopped Duncan had kissed her, full on the mouth. It was a deep and passionate kiss, more than she expected, and even though she pulled away from him slightly, his tongue touched her lips and she parted them. It felt very good to open up like this, to open herself up to him. Once the kiss was over they both sat there for a moment, eyes closed. Duncan left a few minutes later, quietly excusing himself because he had a presentation the next morning and Kathryn had a test.

It seemed wrong to part after the fireworks of the kiss, but it also felt right. They could do no wrong—there was a deep connection between them, Kathryn was sure of that.

They officially became an item.

* * *

Both of Duncan's parents had been dead for some time. His mother died when he was seven in a car accident (a drunk driver); his father died of a heart attack then he was twenty-five. He had two brothers, Sean, who was three years older, and Thomas, who was one year, to the day, younger. His younger sister, Jennifer, had recently turned thirty. He had one niece, by Jennifer, named

Angela, who was two. None of them had spoken to each other, or cared to, for over a year. They scarcely spoke after their father died—he was the glue that kept the family together. The only real time they got together was after Angela was born. There were cards at Christmas and birthdays, but nothing else. So when the time came to meet the family, there was only one to meet.

Kathryn had one sister, Tamara, who was two years older than she and had always been the favorite. She had always gotten As in school, while Kathryn had gotten mostly Bs and Cs, and was a star athlete. Kathryn had always been reserved and not at all interested in sports of any kind, focusing on art more than popularity. She had gone to art school in California for one year, but it was too expensive, and she missed home, so she went to Barnesville University, majoring in English and Psychology. She also planned on getting a teaching degree. She passed all her classes, but no one in her family was much impressed. They were never much impressed with anything Kathryn did. Bringing home a man sixteen years older than she did cause a bit of a stir.

It did not go well.

Although Duncan was charming, intelligent, and sharply dressed, her family was hostile from the minute they walked in. Her father, a construction worker since he was fifteen, thought Duncan was too high class to really appreciate her; her mother, a school secretary, thought she was giving her youth away by getting too serious with Duncan too fast. Her sister, as usual, was indifferent, but she made sure to highlight her boyfriend of over a year, the Barnesville Badger's star quarterback. Her sister's relationship was the real deal, Kathryn's just a trick, a pipe dream. These hard, get-used-to-it facts were voiced within the first five minutes.

It did not go well at all; Kathryn and Duncan left before they finished dinner. It did, however, cement Kathryn's feelings for

Duncan, and his for her. In fact, her feelings for him only increased by the minute.

* * *

Within a few weeks they were talking about moving in together. There was a tangible feeling of "us against the world" between them, and living together seemed a logical, though modern move. Kathryn, bring old fashioned, declined—for the time being. It just didn't seem right. They decided to continue as they were and see what would happen.

* * *

Every day until their one-year anniversary when Kathryn woke she would turn off the alarm and turn on the light in one swift motion. Then she would stare at the picture of Duncan she had on her nightstand for a few minutes. There were two pictures in the frame: one was a smiling Duncan in a baseball shirt and jeans taken at a company softball game, the other was much smaller and lodged into the corner. It was a small picture of the two of them taken on their second date. Duncan had taken it with his camera phone and printed it off his computer for her. He could have given her a regular sized picture, but Kathryn did not like to look at herself, not even in the mirror to make sure her hair was fixed, and decided that a small version would be fine. All she really wanted was a photo of them together—proof. She still couldn't believe that something as marvelous as Duncan was happening to her, and the picture reminded her that it was indeed happening, and best of all, to her. The thought gave her a not-so-unpleasant warm feeling in her stomach.

PREDILECTION

After that she would shower, do her make-up, which she had only began wearing regularly once she and Duncan got "serious," and get dressed. Most days she dressed a little fancier than she normally would have, on the off chance she and Duncan would get together for a quick lunch or something. Then she would eat her breakfast and wait for Duncan to call—he always called her before she went to class.

It was never more than a, "how are you doing? Have a great day" quickie conversation, but it reassured her, and she found she looked forward to it more than she would admit. Whether or not Duncan knew she waited for the call, sometimes just sitting there staring at the wall until the phone rang, she couldn't tell.

Then she would go to class and sit absentmindedly thinking of Duncan. More often than not she sat in the back of the class so no one would see she wasn't taking notes. (Duncan helped her study for exams—the only reason she passed that year.) Usually she dreamt of their past dates or happy moments. Sometimes she began to plan their wedding (which had never been more than lightly discussed, really, glossed over), sometimes she thought of names for their children (unborn and still very far away); other times she thought of Duncan in individual pieces—the way his hair flipped out behind his ears and how when light struck it just right it seemed to be a little reddish; his eyes, his long, slender fingers with perfectly cut and shaped nails, his toned body (especially when he wore his fitted men's dress shirts—the black or red one, sleeves rolled up just below his elbows—Jesus); how tall and how long his legs looked when he wore the one pair of faded jeans, how great he looked in all his other pants, his smile. She thought of him naked, wondered what it would feel like to have his skin against hers, how it would look if he were on top of her, smiling. No matter what else she dwelt on, she always thought of his smile—perfectly aligned little, white, slippery teeth and how his eyes lit up ever so slightly.

She was sure they would be together forever.

Duncan grew fonder of Kathryn every day. Each time she spoke he found new wisdom in her words, and they always had a good laugh. He really enjoyed her company—the more time he spent with her the more he missed her when she was away. He knew she was a little overzealous, sometimes waiting for him to call on pins and needles, scolding him if he was even the slightest bit late, like she couldn't stand one more second without him. He felt most of the same for her, that constant, but enjoyable, need to be with her, so he let it go. He never dismissed her because of her age—to him it didn't matter and he couldn't really tell anyway—but he excused her excessive enthusiasm because she was, after all, only twenty-one. In truth, her abundance of passion excited him, hasty or otherwise.

He also grew more attracted to her by leaps and bounds. They had not had sex. Kathryn had refused (she had revealed to him after about a month that she was still a virgin; she had only kissed and held hands with guys, nothing more), and although at times it was nerve-wracking he ultimately respected her even more for it. It also made her seem unattainable, which was very enticing itself; on the other hand, she was his, which made him feel like a champion, and that was a great feeling. They were also intellectual equals in most respects, although Kathryn slacked a lot in her studies, which he had never done. She also shared his same sense of humor—very dry, sarcastic, but also appreciative of the ridiculous.

He also trusted her completely. Whenever he had an idea for advertisements, he ran it by her first, relying on her opinion; he came to her with any problems. He felt he could totally give himself to her—he felt free with her. He had begun dating at seventeen, and in his two decades of experience no one had ever made him feel like Kathryn did.

He was sure they would be together forever.

* * *

The night of their one-year anniversary, October 10, was different from minute one. There was some sort of electricity in the air, brushing Kathryn's face like the breeze. Excitement crackled between them when they met at the same restaurant they dined at on their first date.

During dessert Duncan presented Kathryn with a bouquet of roses. The card had a huge, square diamond ring attached to it. He got down on one knee, and asked her to be his wife. She eagerly accepted. The other people in the restaurant cheered and clapped.

That night, once he had gone home, she sat on her bed, staring at the gorgeous carats adorning her finger, and cried from the overwhelming happiness she felt.

Fragmentation

The only question now was when to get married and how. Neither could decide if they needed to do it quickly, no-frills, or pull out all the stops in a lavish ceremony months, or years, down the road. A big wedding would be a celebration of their love, one giant party, which they both liked the notion of, but a tiny wedding would be intimate and private in keeping with the way they always were. They were very quiet about their relationship to the few who asked.

They decided to make it official between the two of them and a justice of the peace. They could always have a party later.

Within three weeks they were married.

Duncan drove nearly 70 on the back roads of Barnesville to get to his house: no, *their* house. They had begun moving Kathryn's things into his house bit by bit as soon as they decided on when to marry. They had moved in everything but an overnight suitcase of the essentials. Kathryn spent the last night of their engagement at her apartment, even though her futon was no longer there; she had slept on a few thick blankets on the floor—she refused to live with him for even one second if they weren't man and wife. Her suitcase was now in the backseat.

They arrived at the white three-story house built on a hill. It looked to be two-stories from the road, but the hill concealed the third level, and once the car was parked they jumped out and ran to the door, Duncan behind Kathryn, pulling at the bottom of her white skirt, playfully chasing her. At the door, Duncan grabbed Kathryn, kissed her as deeply as he could, and picked her up. He carried her into the house, kicked the door shut, took her up the staircase, and led her into the bedroom.

He sat her down on the bed and went to shut the door. He turned around and his mouth dropped open. He had thought he would need to lead the way for her, to teach her, but she was standing at the foot of the bed stark naked.

He looked up and down the curves of her body, and undressed as he went to her. She came up to him and undressed him herself, greedily unbuttoning his shirt, taking off his belt, and pulling down his pants. He watched her slide off his briefs; she looked up at him with hungry eyes and licked her lips. He pulled her up to him, kissed her, and carried her to the bed, her legs wrapped around his waist.

They became man and wife completely.

* * *

Kathryn decided that her new home needed a makeover. She loved it, but it still resembled a bachelor pad. The bedroom had already been changed from simple white walls and beige carpet to red walls, red and black patterned curtains, and a large maroon, white, and black rug that covered almost all of the carpet. They were going to repaint and put in new carpet, but they decided to put in hardwood floors, tile, and paint. The bathrooms were painted light blue and mint green, except for the master bath, which was more than double the size of the other two; it was done in white and black, with the floor checkerboard tile. The rest of the house was either given a new coat of cream-colored paint and stayed the same, or done in shades of red and black. Duncan let Kathryn do whatever she wanted to the house. Once they were married he gave her everything she asked for.

Their lives became steady; they settled into a routine. It was surprisingly hard to live with someone else, especially getting used to all their habits that you didn't like. They both made an effort to work at it. They developed a schedule they stuck to almost exclusively, but they also tried to be spontaneous. Soon Kathryn began her spring semester and Duncan had a few new clients. Kathryn quit her job at the day care to focus on school and, on another level, ease into becoming a housewife. They planned to have a big family, and once Kathryn had her degree they would start trying for children. Both secretly hoped the children would come earlier than they planned, and their love life reflected it.

Throughout the course of their relationship, Kathryn had always been less independent than Duncan had. She had always seemed to need him; seemed to need to need him. Once they married it became even worse. It seemed to Duncan that her insecurities had only deepened. He had hoped a permanent commitment would put her mind at ease, but it became clear Kathryn was sinking deeper and deeper into herself.

At first she had just clung to him, but slowly her behavior became smothering. Soon she had escalated into full-blown madness. She had stopped going to class after a few weeks; within a month she nearly refused to leave the house without him. She had a strict schedule of when he had to call her just to check in. If a meeting ran over, or he lost track of time, or just forgot, she would be nearly hysterical once he did call. After a few weeks, if he didn't call, she would call him until he answered. Near the beginning of March, after four months of marriage, he began to keep track of the calls. One day he purposely did not call her, and she rang him nearly 30 times, each about two minutes apart, before he finally answered. She was crying.

"I thought something horrible had happened to you! Don't do that to me!" was all she had said, and hung up.

He had tried to talk to her, to see what had caused her to retreat. There had not be any apparent reason for her to basically become a hermit. They rarely fought, they had a great sex life, even after Kathryn began to become depressed, and as far as he knew her schooling had been going well. She had even completed enough classes, through night and summer school, to graduate a semester early, which factored into their getting married so soon.

But then she tried to get Duncan to quit his job. She needed him with her, she said. At first she tried to keep him with sex, and it worked—once, because every man needs to take off sick at least one day in his life so he can devote all his energies to pleasing his wife. But Duncan would not touch her once he realized she was only playing him.

There were a few days, near the beginning of her refusal to leave the house, that he had taken off of work to stay with her but she would not give anything up. She kept whatever was bothering her to herself. Anything else you wanted to ask her, she would tell, but ask her why Duncan could not be out of her sight, and she would cry and lock herself in the bathroom.

Eventually, Duncan went back to work. He felt horrible about it, leaving her alone in their big house, but he had to work.

Duncan decided to confront her. This had to stop. He got the names of several reputable therapists from his Employee Assistance Program and planned to have Kathryn pick one and start seeing him immediately. He wanted her to get help so he could have his wife back. He could tell when he looked at her that her life had slowly become a prison, and he did not want to be a part of that. He decided that Kathryn would either get help or he was leaving. He would not help her lose her life for no reason. He loved her too much to stand aside while she tore herself apart.

He had no idea Kathryn was already in shreds.

Annihilation

Kathryn did not really know what had taken over her. All she knew was an incredible feeling of need; she responded to it. She tried not to give in to that feeling, she tried so hard, desperately, but fighting it was too hard—it began to consume her. It was as if a survival mechanism within her had been switched on. The need to not be alone was overwhelming. She was scared to be alone, even though now she was not. She had a lifelong companion, but it was not enough. It seemed that the loneliness within her had gripped her mind with its claws and twisted the soft flesh. She had always been a loner, but now she rebelled against it. Duncan was her only way out of whatever it was that she was drowning in.

In her own mind, the justification for what she planned to do was simple: she had to get rid of this feeling, this horrendous low she found herself submerged in, and whatever she had to do to get out she would. She didn't want to feel this way, and she didn't want to hurt Duncan. She wanted him to live, to respond to her, to thrive with her, forever as her husband, to give her children and to raise them with her, to die with him.

She had tried to convince herself that she was wrong, that

Duncan would not leave, that the happiness would stay in her life. But when someone has never really known happiness, even the faintest glimpse of it is torture because pain is the easiest thing to give in to, and live in, but the hardest thing to conquer.

Duncan was everything to her, and that was the key to her only way out.

Her excruciating indifference, pain, and joy centered on Duncan. She couldn't live with him if this feeling would stay, but she couldn't live without him. Something had to be done.

* * *

When Duncan got home that night, he had the list of local therapists folded in his suit-coat pocket. He decided he would be kind, but firm, at first, and if she didn't bite he would give her the ultimatum. He wished it wouldn't come to that.

The front door was open, which was unusual for Kathryn. Even when she had been in her right mind—it pained him to think that; she really wasn't the same woman anymore—she always had the doors locked and windows closed, curtains drawn.

"Kathryn," he called. No answer.

He went down the front hall to the living room. She wasn't there. The oven was on, he could smell the gas. There was spaghetti inside, warming. The dining room table was set, two red candles lit in the middle. There was something else on the table as well—a note. It was watermarked from tears.

Duncan:

I realize I haven't been myself lately. But I've done some thinking, and I think I know how I can get better. I'll need your help. I'm sorry for how I've acted. I'm so, so sorry. You deserve better and I can only hope you'll forgive me.

I want to make it up to you.
I've got a surprise for you—upstairs.

I'm so, so sorry.

Kathryn

He immediately went to the bedroom. There was a path of red rose petals from the top stair to their bedroom. The door was closed, but he could see light flickering under it. He opened the door, slowly; there were candles everywhere. There had to be fifty. They were on the nightstands, the dresser, the windowsill, on the floor. The rose petals were scattered in a circle around the bed. Kathryn was in the middle of it, posed like an Egyptian queen, her long hair draped over her shoulders. She had on his favorite negligee, the pink lace one, and strapped pink heels. She smiled at him and beckoned him with her finger. She turned onto her back and he saw as he came to her, taking off his coat, that she did not have on panties. He laid his coat across the hope chest that lay at the foot of the bed. It was the only piece of furniture, apart from the bed, without candles on it.

They kissed for a long time. It felt like all the tension between them was being released, and they sank into each other. It felt like their minds were becoming one. Kathryn broke from him, and slithered away, slowly, her hips high in air, to the end of the bed.

"The surprise is in here," she whispered, reaching into the chest and pulling out a pair of handcuffs. Duncan moaned softly. Kathryn crawled back to him, sinking her chest lower than she needed to so he would look at it. She kissed her way up his body, straddled him, and secured him to the bed.

"I love you," she said, and then told him she had another surprise. Duncan took in a sharp breath. This was *amazing*. He looked at her admiringly as she worked her way back down his body and then into to the hope chest. What could she possibly be getting out? He slipped into thoughts so dirty he was ashamed to think them. He only withdrew from his haze when he realized Kathryn was standing beside him. He completely snapped back to reality when he realized she was crying.

There was a hammer in her hand.

She whispered a choked, "I'm so sorry...I love you," and raised her arm. Duncan had always wondered if death hurt. Is there pain with death when you know it's coming? Duncan saw her raise the hammer, felt the slightest agony, and then there was only black.

Kathryn went downstairs, wiping the red dots from her face, not realizing they became streaks across her face, thickened because it was all over her hands as well. She took the candles from the dining room table and lit all the curtains on the first floor with them. She returned to the bedroom, slowly going up the stairs, thinking of when she and Duncan had first met, their first date, their wedding; she tried to push out the images of him crushed, the bloodied pillow, from her mind. She knocked over all the candles she had painstakingly set up earlier, curled up next to Duncan on the bed, and cried. *This fire will purify*, she thought.

She let the flames consume everything.

Nefarious

To Autumn—thank you.

My name is Andrew Smith. Not a spectacular name, I know; quite ordinary, in fact, though not as clichéd as if my first name were John. I live in a small apartment in a small Midwestern town. I have a college degree and a decent job. My parents have been married for nearly thirty years; I suffered none of the usual childhood traumas. I had lots of friends in school; I have plenty of friends now. I eat a nutritionally balanced diet, bathe regularly, brush and floss two or three times a day, drink limited amounts of alcohol, don't smoke, and get seven to eight hours of sleep a night. I have a healthy, stable, normal life. What bothers me is that I am so goddamned unhappy.

That thought may not be so unusual, but it has that nagging, pulling throb that just drives you crazy. I live my entire life in that throb: dull, pulsing breaths and slow, steady heartbeats. Everything seems to be in slow motion. It's the sluggishness that I have trouble with, the numbness all the stillness causes. It's a lot like suffocating.

In an attempt to cheer me up, my parents took me fishing. There's this farm a few hours south of town, near my grandparents', a farm that belongs to a friend of theirs; it has a large lake and a dock to fish from. Seeing as I try not leave my house unless it's absolutely vital, I was not sure how this was supposed to lift my spirits.

The drive to this farm is a bore. There's nothing but highway, trees, and fields for two hours, a side road here or there, maybe an old farmhouse you glimpse fleetingly. The big event is when the road curves to the right, an off-ramp, and you go through the nearest "big" town: it has a McDonald's and a grocery store, so you know it's the center of high lifestyle. After that, there's nothing but lonely road again.

We stopped at my grandparents' for a quick visit before we set about our grand afternoon. I love my grandparents very much, let me just say that. They are two of the sweetest, most generous, funny, great people I know. They keep me laughing, mostly for their naivety, their childlike enthusiasm. But they are also old, so they have a sleepy quality to them and repeat themselves a lot; my grandmother is not happy unless you're eating. It is actually enjoyable to visit them. However, this did not make me want to go fishing any more than I already did; it only made me dread it. I had a ham sandwich, at my grandmother's behest, even though I wasn't hungry, and we left, two bags of chips and a store bought apple pie in tow ("there's just no way we can eat them; you go ahead and take it," my grandmother insisted).

It took about five minutes to get to the farm. The road we took was bumpy and made my head swim a bit. Luckily I didn't feel the need to puke. We pulled into the long dirt driveway and drove around the house and main barn. There was no one home. A dog greeted us with a few curious and loud barks and ran, its tail wagging, following our car. We drove over the yard, through the grass, some of it recently cut, some still tall like weeds. We parked near the lake and climbed out of the car, taking out our tackle box and rods. The smell of freshly cut grass welcomed us, mixed with that unmistakable smell of the outdoors—air, pollen, animals. My mom and dad had already walked onto the dock; I had been looking around, taking it all in. Behind us was a fenced-in piece of land, mostly dust and dirt, occupied by a small doghouse and miniature barn.

My dad called to me, "Watch for the male turkey—he's big and black, and if you're not careful, he'll attack you." *Oh, great.* I could hear him gobbling loudly somewhere behind me.

All around us, beyond the rest of the grassy patches, were trees. They were knotted and their limbs skinny, the leaves they had begun to gain in early spring wiped out by the recent cold snap. There were some strange looking birds walking around, some kind of hen, responding to the turkey. They made high pitched, guttural whistles. Birds were chirping in the trees, a rooster was crowing: it was very, very loud. I ventured toward the lake, dismayed that the dock was not too sturdy-looking, joined to the lip of the water, which was rocky, by two pieces of wood laid across it.

My mother: "Just walk across. If it can hold your father and me, it can hold you."

You've got to be kidding me.

I slowly—very slowly, like a tightrope walker—made my way across the slab of wood, feeling it bend and creak below my weight. I sighed to myself once I felt the sturdy wood of the dock beneath me. I stayed close to the edge, not wanting to stray too far from glorious land. The wind was blowing directly at my face, into my eyes. I turned around; a lot of the same. This place was a wind tunnel. It only amplified the noises around me, now punctuated with watery *plops* as our lures penetrated the glossy sheen of the top of the lake.

We kept casting out, coming up empty handed. We decided to go home and see a movie. As we loaded up the car, from within the wind that was rushing in my ears, piercing through the static of the animals, came a scream. It was long, faded at the end, full of pain. It sounded like a man's voice. My eyes widened and my head snapped around. I looked all around me, but didn't see anything. I looked at the trees, but saw only a thicket of sticks.

"Dad, are you ok?" I asked quickly, thinking maybe he had closed the trunk on his fingers—hoping.

"Yeah. Why?" he asked, confused, his eyebrows raised behind his aviator sunglasses. His fingers were fine. He closed the trunk slowly, locking it with his key.

"Nothing," I replied quickly, and got into the car.

It was all in my imagination. It had to be. What could possibly be causing a scream like that around here? There were no other houses that I could see. I tried to shake away the feeling of uneasiness that had crept into my chest and crawled up my throat. It had to be my imagination. As we drove back to the road, I took one last look around—the trees beckoning me to step inside, knotted mouths and eyes.

I wish I had never looked back.

* * *

It started slowly, as most wretched things do. The only way someone can become consumed by something is for it to latch itself into the subconscious and then slip insidiously into every other crack and crevasse of the mind until there is nothing left. No one is ever overwhelmed all at once. Even in a rage or passion, the underlying feeling was already there. There is always a basis for these things, and unfortunately, when you don't understand the basis—when you don't understand your own feelings—there is no way you can hope to stop the madness. There is no turning back if you don't know where you came from.

The point of no return, for me, was marked with a giant red X. There was no mistaking it, but at the time I only vaguely registered what was happening. I saw it, walked right on by, and looked back to wave. Maybe I wanted to walk away.

After we went fishing, we drove back home and saw a movie—the latest animated film that was made to happily please both adults and children. It actually wasn't that bad. Throughout the ride home, the ride to the movies, the revolving screens of useless trivia and awful music, the new movie previews, the movie itself, I was distracted, hopelessly so. I could not get my mind off that scream. It had been so primal, so purely articulate. It seemed I had heard that scream somewhere before. Either that or it just kept echoing in my head so it seemed like the scream had existed there before. There suddenly seemed to be so many gray areas in my life, so many inconsistencies that I was now unexpectedly, entirely indifferent to.

The next day, all I could think about was that scream. It was just one sound, seconds long. The mystery behind it, the possibility of the damage that may have unfolded—all the possibilities flaunted themselves in front of me; I could see them flickering behind my eyes as I looked in the mirror, tiny vapors. I sat on the edge of my bed that next night, staring into space. I don't know how long I sat there, but when I finally pulled my legs under the covers I noticed my clock said it was quarter after three. I had very strange dreams.

After I woke up, I went to work; I'm a manager at a local department store. I went through the motions, looking at sales figures, making sure every customer was greeted and helped when needed. I kept our inventory and shelves in top shape. I answered the telephone and worked the cash register in slow swipes. I went through the motions, bit by bit. Monotony can be a great cover.

I drove home in my fuel efficient little car, the radio blaring, trying to drown out the thoughts in my head. I picked up some Chinese take out, ate it in my living room, TV on, another repeat of a sitcom I had seen a million times before. I brushed my teeth and went to bed as soon as I could let myself without feeling like I was doing my youth some great disservice. I slept restlessly. I had very strange dreams.

* * *

Day four, since I happened to be keeping count, began as normally as any other day. I woke up when my alarm began buzzing that unholy noise that trumpets through my brain, and immediately turned the alarm off and rolled over to go back to sleep. After a few more minutes dozing, I got up and shambled into the bathroom. I looked back at the bed and wondered if I had had a bad night: I had kicked off all my covers, and distantly remembered waking up briefly, broken out in a cold sweat. I went back to sleep before I even registered what had happened— another one of those nightmares I'd been having.

They were all different, the nightmares, but all centered on some kind of monster. Maybe it was human, its face was distinctly blank, like white slate, but its body was hulking, veins protruding and pulsing, skin bloody red and crusty yellow-green. It may have had hair; I'm not sure. No matter what it was nasty, and whenever it opened its mouth, out came the scream that had been haunting me, like rumbling thunder smacking into lightning.

As I remembered the dream and the sweat, I walked past the bathroom mirror to get to the toilet. As I moved past it, the overhead light flickered as it struggled to stay on—I should have replaced it days ago. My reflection caught my eye. There was something wrong with my face. I looked in the mirror for a long time, finding myself unable to place what the discrepancy was. I pulled at my eyelids, tugged and scratched at my hair. I felt the stubble on my chin; there was nothing out of the ordinary. That was when I realized the problem was not with my face: it was my neck.

A patch of skin on the left side was dry and flaky, maybe even a little yellow.

It itched like crazy, that constant, irritating, almost stinging kind of itch, the kind that only really registers in your subconscious, like the nerves themselves are exposed, and before you can stop yourself you've scratched it raw. The area was only about the size of a quarter, but it was enough.

In the back of my mind I heard that scream, over and over again, like a skipping record. I showered and dressed, leaving my razor untouched because I had the strange feeling that if I picked it up, I would shave the itchy patch of skin instead of just scratching. I could picture the blood running down my neck, bright against the white of the sink, the pink-yellow stains that would remain on the porcelain for years to come. And then I thought about taking the razor and slitting my own throat. I imagined how the blood would rise from the cut, and begin to pour down my front, my neck opened with a second mouth, gums black with blood.

It was very strange—I could see it all very clearly, how it would look, smell, feel—and I wasn't disturbed by it until much later. I pictured my own injury, my own death, most likely, and I felt nothing.

* * *

I went to work, made it listlessly throughout the day. Quite a few people commented on my rough patch of skin, all of them giving me some sort of remedy on how to fix it. A lot of them involved lotion; one involved honey, lemon juice, and sandpaper. I turned my collar up and left it that way for the rest of the day.

After work I stopped at the local quick-fix, we-have-ten-of-everything-you-could-ever-want store and bought a bottle of lotion. I hoped it would help the dry patch of skin. Then I bought some allergy medicine to stop the itching. I ate some fast food for dinner, if you could call it that, and went to bed because the medicine knocked me back a few days.

I had the dream again; this time the scream did come from a face: my own.

* * *

When I woke up in the morning the rough patch had grown. It had spread in all directions; it looked like an odd-shaped pool. The skin that had been yellow and crusty was now reddened and wet, like the blood was right under the surface. The skin seemed thin and stretched tight, the main vein underneath it sticking out, blue and swollen.

Needless to say—although I don't know why anyone says that if the next thought it so obvious, but—I was not in a particularly good mood. In fact, besides being concerned over this spreading rough patch, and a little annoyed over it, I wasn't feeling too well. I was very tired and achy. I also felt like my entire neck was on fire, inside and out. I cleared my throat several times as soon as I woke up, reflexively, but it didn't help. Later, when I saw what the patch looked like and touched the rash, if that was what it was, I had to be very gentle because it hurt like hell; it was also very hot. I actually had to pull my fingertips away because of the heat. My eyes burned. I was so tired. When I took my temperature it was

104°. I knew that was bad but didn't care. Let me brain melt, let it burn up into a congealed jelly mess.

I called off work and went back to bed. I just could not face whatever was happening. I couldn't bring myself to even think about it. This was too strange and spreading, escalating too quickly. Just sleep it off, I thought to myself, just ignore the problem completely. I was so tired.

As I slept, I had dreams like I'd never had before—not dreams really, more like *visions*. I could see the farm where I heard the scream, the lake water rippling in the wind. The trees were swaying, their leaves a sickly brown color. Then suddenly I was inside a tree, hidden among the branches, staring down over the lake. The only feeling I had was that I absolutely did not want to look down. *Don't look into the water.* As I looked around me, I realized the leaves that engulfed me weren't colored a deadened brown—they were covered in blood.

Don't look into the water.

Luckily it was the weekend. This thing, this condition, whatever the hell it was, I didn't really care, was cramping my style. It was throwing off my routine, one thing I do not take kindly to. I am very set in my ways, stubborn, and when I don't get to do the things I normally do—which by the time they become a part of my schedule are things I really just *want* but my brain says I *need* to do—I get very cranky. I'm unpleasant to be around. Without work hanging over my head, although I hold my job as a priority, I could focus on my disfigurement. What the hell was wrong with me?

My own stupidity was the cause of most of my trouble. If I had gone to the doctor instead of sleeping the whole day when I took off work, I would not have gotten into this mess. If I had gotten my act together instead of doing what I wanted, which was to just close my eyes to the problem and sleep, sleep, sleep, I'd have some answers. But now I was stuck with myself and my stupid self-indulgences and stuck without a doctor.

I could go to the emergency room but those places are definitely some form of purgatory. Not only do you have to pay at least $50 a pop—if you've got insurance—but then you have to wait for hours on end to get someone to take care of you. And the people you have to sit with are a real side-show. There're people bleeding everywhere and snot-nosed kids squalling; people rambling to themselves or too loudly to the person next to them in some language you don't know, probably talking about what a freak you are. Not to mention the horrid medical care. Once I saw a guy with two broken legs have to wait three hours to see a doctor. You could see the bone in his ankle sticking out a bit but the guy with a sore throat got to go first.

The skin on your neck turning to mush is an emergency in my book, but you never know with doctors. So I decided I'd take my chances doing some investigating on my own.

As all scholars do, I started with the internet. All search engines give variations of the same sites, so you can envision me using whichever one you prefer. I started with a search of my symptoms, in the simplest form: skin rash and fever. The first website I came to was a particularly useful one that consisted of a series of yes and no questions concerning my rash. The questions were printed in boxes, with arrows leading you to another box with another question if you answered "no" or to a description of your ailment if it was a "yes." It was like a guess and check board game, actually quite fun. The closest results I could find all related to skin cancer or a fungal infection. None of them really fit the bill.

The next website gave me the definition of "rash"—as if no one knows what that is—and then a list of rashes to sift through to find the right one. For such a simplistic beginning it became awfully complicated. No thanks. The third website was similar.

Finally I came across a "medical" website. I'd seen commercials for it on TV but I was not impressed. There were pictures of the different rashes, which were helpful, but none of the ones described spread and changed as much as mine did and none of the pictures really looked like my rash. After a few hours of much of the same, I gave up.

I decided to sit around for the rest of the day watching television, flipping between crappy cable specials about what was great about certain decades, year by year, countdowns of the best music videos of the week (which is really the same as last week and the week before that), reality competitions, and a few maybe worthwhile specials about history, as well as food challenge competitions—those are awesome. I sat around for almost four hours just staring at the screen, laughing at some things, not really enthralled or entertained but just taking up time. I sat in my boxers and a t-shirt, eating chips and drinking soda.

I took a break to eat; put some pants on and drove through a fast food joint. The value menu, most items priced below a dollar, is one of the greatest ideas of modern man. People know the health dangers and unsanitary conditions of fast food, so interest is somewhat waning; how do we bring them back? The answer: make it cheap. You'll die from a heart attack in a few years, but hey, think of all the money you'll save!

All the while, I could feel the rash, the disease. It was always there, in a way subconsciously, under the surface. I could feel the slight pulse of the protruding vein; feel the pull of the taut skin, the itch that had turned into a burning nerve, like it was dying. My throat was scratchy, like I was constantly thirsty. No amount of water or soda could quench my thirst. The hoarseness made it uncomfortable to swallow, the kind of discomfort that gets interpreted as pain, but it's really not. A sore throat, maybe, I couldn't be sure. My head was always hurting, dully. The headache really came and went, sometimes a hard pounding, like a sledgehammer, sometimes barely noticeable; but it was always there. My eyes burned from the fever that spiked and lowered, but never quite made it back down to a normal temperature. My fingers were heavy, like they were swollen and asleep, thick and hard to move. My arms and legs were heavy as well. I was slow; above all, I was just so tired.

No, above all—there was the itch. I knew the rash was there, spreading slowly but definitely progressively, and that made the itch worse. I could mostly ignore it, but it was always there, irritating, inviting me to scratch away. But it was so wet I wouldn't dare. I waned to, badly, dig my nails in and rip down, just to make the awful itching *stop*.

I aimlessly drove back home, not seeing the drive, just making the motions. When I pulled into the driveway, I had no recollection of how I got there. I tried to shake off that absent sinking feeling it gave me and took my greasy bag and paper cup inside. I kicked off my shoes, which were barely on to begin with, ripped off my jogging pants, laughing to myself—it was, I admit, fun to rip the snaps free, like some stripper or something. Then I sat back down in front of the TV, chewing big, dripping bites of my packed cheeseburger, like a cow, my cheeks packed full. To help force it down, I sucked up some soda, whetting the whole mess. I ate my fries with abandon, savoring the salt as I licked it from my fingertips. I must have been a disgusting display—but hey, it only cost me three dollars for the whole meal.

I looked down at my shirt, feeling wet on my chest. I realized

I had spilt not ketchup, but blood. I threw the remnants of my dinner onto the couch cushion beside me and stumbled hurriedly into the bathroom. I threw the door open, the knob smacking hard against the wall with a loud metal thump. The lights seemed very bright; they hurt my eyes and I had to squint. That's what I can remember about the next few moments; they're a blur, like I've lost them, but I can remember the squinting and how I had to work out, in my panic, exactly what I saw. I had to figure it out, because I couldn't comprehend what I was seeing, couldn't believe it.

The disease had spread, and I was bleeding a lot from the wound. I used a towel to stop the bleeding, sopping it all up, the towel a wet mess in my hands. This was a disease, not a rash, I now knew for certain. This was no fungal rash or cancer. Cancer doesn't rot away your flesh.

After I bandaged my neck, covering the showing muscle, visible tendons flexing and all, I went to put the towel I had used into the washing machine. When I looked down at it as I dropped it into the soapy water, I saw it was covered in not only blood, but also skin. It floated in the water, moving back and forth. I had taken off all the skin of my neck as I sopped up the blood, in one large chunk. I stared at the washing machine in dazed horror, watching the water turn pink. My dream from the night before came back to me.

I went into my bedroom, sat on the edge of the bed, and wept.

* * *

My head had already been pounding, but on Sunday, the pound had turned into a deep throb, like my entire brain was pulsating; it was the headache that woke me up. I had been asleep for thirteen hours. I don't think I had moved the entire time, because I thought my knees and elbows were going to pop, break, and leave the lower half of my extremities hanging lifelessly. I was fairly sure I had dreamed during the night, but I could only vaguely recall the feeling of dreaming, not the actual dreams. It was the first night since I had heard the scream that was dreamless. Or so I hoped.

My neck was no better. The huge gauze pads I had covered the exposed muscle with were soaked brown with blood. The tape was curled in at the edges, revealing red, irritated skin. I couldn't tell if that was a reaction to the tape or the spreading of the plague that had begun to grip me.

I changed the bandage, pulling off the thin layer of new skin that had formed. I tried to hold back the pain, but couldn't. I grunted back a scream as I pulled it off slowly; it felt like a hard rip. The hurt took my breath away, and I stood half bent over, my hands on my knees and head lowered in the middle of the bathroom, coughing and breathing in shallow gasps. As I heaved, I could feel the muscles in my neck pulling and releasing, like every nerve was exposed, sending bolts of pain through me, like my neck was being sliced repeatedly with knives of fire. My eyes began to water, almost like I was crying. A sudden wave of nausea came over me and I fell to my knees. Once I regained myself I bandaged the wound again and changed clothes, not bothering to shower or shave. I went back into my living room and watched TV for a few more hours. Then I called off work for the next two days, went back to bed, and slept.

When I woke up in the morning I felt as if I had spent the last week in a drunken stupor and now had the worst hangover of all time. My eyes were dry, my throat ached, my temples pounded. I thought about calling the people that keep world records and seeing if there was any way they could measure the amount of pain I was in and put my name in for consideration; I was sure I would make the next publication. I went into the bathroom to make my now-daily check of my wound.

The disease had taken over half of my neck.

I no longer registered the pain as I removed the bandages; the pure shock I felt at seeing what had happened underneath them left me bewildered. As I looked in the mirror at the disfigurement that was overcoming me, I knew there was no stopping it. It was only a matter of time before this thing—whatever it was—completely consumed me. Thinking back, I knew what was coming. Maybe I began planning for…later events…at that moment.

It was at about this time that my mother called. I have always felt that the telephone is a great invention, but should have a better appearance. The ring of a telephone, for example, is horrific. That sound is so grating it compels the people around it to pick it up, not because they are curious to speak to whoever is calling, but because they want that damn ring to stop. When the phone rang the sound alone threw me into a frenzy, like a switch had been flipped. My nerves were frayed, and the harsh noise of the phone pushed me over the edge. I picked up the receiver enraged, full-fisted, winced as the slight muscle movement of the arm motion sent a shockwave through my neck.

I grunted out, "What?"

"Hi, Andy, sweetheart, it's me," my mother's cheery voice greeted me. She was always so pleasant; even when things were bad my mother was always smiling and comforting. She was unrelenting in her staunch support of me. When I was a child, if I was sick she would always stay home with me, fawning over me and taking me to the doctor, nursing me back to health with kind words and full-toothed smiles. When I heard her voice I wanted to cry: I needed that smile right now, needed her hand to brush back the hair from my fevered forehead and give me soup. The sound of her voice made me want to bawl. God, I missed her.

"How are you doing? It's been a while since we've heard from you; we were just a little worried."

"I'm fine, Mom," I lied.

I had been living on my own since my eighteenth birthday. I had wanted to prove to my parents that I was adult enough to make it out in the cold world all by myself. They had been reluctant, but I had enough money to pay the rent and eat so they let me go. Both of them had expected me back within six months. I never did. There were months were I ate nothing but bread and water, maybe some eggs if I could find them for cheap or maybe those thin sugar wafer cookies that cost a dollar, but I always played the tough guy. I acted like nothing was wrong; I could handle it. And I did. Eventually my shifts at work picked up, I got promoted, and could afford to eat meat. Shortly after that I could afford to move into a bigger apartment in a better neighborhood.

This time in my life was worse than any other, but I wasn't about to ask for help now. I couldn't show any weakness, so I just turned myself off, shut down. Up went the wall.

"Are you sure? What have you been up to lately? We went to your work the other day, but you weren't there...."

"I took the day off because I wasn't feeling well." A bit of an understatement.

"Are you sick? What's wrong? Did you go to the doctor?" She said all three questions in the space of a single second; I could tell her mom antennae had detected my untruthfulness. Moms always know.

"Yeah, Mom, I'm fine. It was just a temporary thing; maybe twenty-four hour flu or something."

"Do you feel all right now?"

"Mom, I'm *fine.*"

"Did you go to the doctor? You know how you always have a hard time getting better once—"

"Dammit, Mom, I said I'm fine! What part of that don't you fucking understand?"

I snapped. No, I didn't snap; I broke. I completely lost my cool, mostly because I could not let her think there was something wrong with me, and her nagging questions, only out of loving concern, made me want to choke her. Choke that little voice out completely—that little voice that was in my mind, telling me to do the right thing. I yelled at her at the top of my lungs.

"I'm fine Mom! I don't need to go to the doctor and I don't need your help. I am fine without you so just leave me the fuck alone!"

I had never even cursed in my mother's presence, let alone at her. The phone replied stunned silence to me. Instead of deterring my emotions, it was like the floodgates opened. I really could not control myself anymore.

"I don't need your help, you understand? Just leave me the hell alone, you and Dad! Got it? I don't need you—I never did!"

I slammed down the phone and then disconnected the cord from the phone jack and punched the wall in one swift moment. It left a pretty nice dent.

It also used the muscles in my neck and shoulder. It felt like I ripped my shoulder out—not out of the socket, but completely out of my body. Like I could look down at the floor and see my entire arm lying there. I looked down for a moment and saw the floor rushing at my face as I passed out.

The next day I decided to suck it up, dip into my savings, and go to the doctor. Within five minutes I was already regretting my decision. The receptionist who answered the phone was a pain in the ass. The receptionists at that office always had been bitches. She answered the phone after just one ring, but then had to put me on hold, because she was so incredibly busy. I sighed to myself, feeling the attempt at a runaround begin, because obviously, the office was not in a buzz and she was not stuck behind a mountain of paperwork and runny noses if she could answer the phone after one ring. But I let her put me on hold for two or three minutes. I told her I needed to make an appointment; she told me the doctor was booked solid for a week.

I tried to press some sense of urgency, but she cut me off and told me curtly if I couldn't wait then maybe I needed to get to the emergency room, where my problem could be addressed more promptly. I then explained my problem to her, as delicately as I could, without being too vulgar, and I don't mean just in my description of my symptoms; I might have let a choice word or two slip in here or there. And amazingly, an available appointment just popped up. I had to be there in an hour.

It took nearly that long to get ready. I had spent most of the last week—no, nearly two now—lounging around my apartment in t-shirts and workout pants or just my boxers. I hadn't shaved, or bathed, only washed my hair a few times. So I had to shower, a major event in itself; I had to try and bathe without getting my neck wet, to save the bandages, although the mess was so wet from blood I wouldn't have been able to differentiate if any water had hit it. I had to shower as quickly as possible because there wasn't much time. I am proud to say I rose to the challenge; I actually managed to do a pretty good job.

I thought about shaving, but decided against it, because there was too much work involved and I was just too tired. Plus, the Grizzly Adams look added to the sense of ill around me. Then I got dressed, if you could call it that: I put on a different pair of workout pants, my red ones since they were clean.

Have you ever tried getting dressed without moving your head and neck? I suggest you try it. Try putting on your pants without being able to see if your feet are going into the legs and having to awkwardly squat to get into them, or lie on the bed and raise your knees to your chest so you can pull the pants over them without having to reach. Try putting on your socks and shoes blindly, try using only your sense of touch. I guess it was kind of like being blind, to draw a physical parallel. Try putting on a shirt, a simple T-shirt, by only moving your arms. It can't be done.

That day, while slipping my shirt over my head, I stretched my neck slightly to force down the edge of the collar, which had gotten stuck on the edge of my ear. Pain shot through me like I had been shot, paralyzing numbness that somehow hurt, shooting down the right side of my body, forcing my down to my knees.

I stayed there, bent crookedly over, my body throbbing, sobbing and heaving, for half an hour. I missed my doctor's appointment. The office did not call to check on me. No one called to check—I had reconnected the phone, but I had told them all to leave me alone, in no uncertain terms. My parents had stopped by the house once to check on me but I didn't answer. In the stillness of my bedroom, accompanied only by the echoing in my head and tears running down my cheeks, I realized I was completely alone.

* * *

I ended up being fired from my job. I had stopped calling in sick, instead spending my time locked in my apartment, sleeping, trying to eat, and trying to fill my mind with distractions from the emptiness that had crawled into my head. After a week of not showing up without notice, the district manager left a message on my answering machine informing me that my last paycheck was in the mail and that if I needed a recommendation not to ask her. Dumb bitch.

The disease had spread over my entire neck. I felt like my head was completely cut off from the rest of my body, suspended in space above my sloped shoulders, hovering over a mess of red-black mush. However, I no longer felt the pain. I had gotten used to it. Or my indifference had completely taken over. Or my nerves were dying.

Whichever; I didn't care.

Before long it covered my entire chest and neck, creeping up to my cheeks like a mangled, clawed hand that stretched its cutting fingers upward toward my eyes.

In less than a month my entire body was covered. Some spots were worse than others. My arms and hands were still useable; the skin had not deteriorated into bloody mush, but a dry and caked, yellow crust. My chest and stomach were slowly being eaten away. Each day the skin became one shade darker red; I could feel the muscle underneath dying, and each day I waited for my stomach to split in two and my intestines spill on the floor, or for my skin to peel off completely and expose my ribcage, my rancid lungs and heart bursting from exposure to the shit that had devoured me.

Actually, that might not have been so bad.

My life had become a void, a vacuum that continually whirled and sucked but didn't benefit me in the slightest. I had consumed everything around me but I still felt empty; it felt like everything I touched, drank, or ate turned the ash. It was like there was a hole in the middle of me I could not fill.

My only solace was sleep. I have always loved to sleep; it's the purest form of escape: drugs, alcohol, no thanks. Sleep is complete and solid. It wraps its satin, hormone arms around your brain and makes everything else disappear. Instead of disabling you it regenerates and is just so…freeing. It's not a dark nothingness; it's a dark hideout where you can release yourself and become nothing. To feel that I did not exist, even for just a moment, was bliss. But soon even that was not enough.

The nightmares I had been having had stopped after the disease began to progress, the worry of seeing its quickness take over. But after a few weeks they returned, more horrific than ever. And once again, they all centered around that scream I had heard on the farm—a sound I had forgotten about until it cleverly crept back into my brain. Then it was all I could think about.

I had to know what was happening to me, and somehow it was connected to that farmhouse. All of this had started after the visit to my grandparents'. All of this had started after that scream echoed out of the forest. I decided to go back there and find out what was going on.

I wish I had never left.

* * *

I slept more peacefully that night; my decision to go back to the farm seemed to have calmed me. There were no nightmares, no scream. There was, however, an itching so bad it woke me in the middle of the night. My right shoulder looked, not bloody and ripped, not diseased and ruined like the rest of my body, but simply caked skin flaking white.

I had this horrible habit of not being able to stop picking at my skin when it was in this condition. If the skin is already peeling off,

I have to remove it. The skin has to be even again. Before, the yellow flaking had come off on its own, bringing blood with it. But now when I brushed it with my palm it flaked a bit, like flecks of dust in the air, but nothing more.

I couldn't resist. It had to come off.

It itched so badly. I had to scratch at it.

It doesn't hurt like you would think it would, pulling off large layers of your own skin. It's actually quite easy and the only discomfort I found was contorting my limbs to be able to reach the deadened skin. I had to twist my arms around my back, or pull my thighs to my chest to reach its underside. To get started you can just brush up the edges, or you might have the use the tip of your nail to push it upward. But then you can pinch it, grab at it with your fingertips, and pull it off. If you're lucky, which I found I was very, once you pull off one piece of skin another small edge will emerge next to where it had been. You can just keep on going and going.

It felt so good.

Even when I saw the blood start to spread, a thin red line that gathered beads and then dripped down slowly, I couldn't stop. It felt so good to get the dead skin off—to remove the disease. I took off as much as I could, almost the entire shoulder and the bottom of my right thigh. An hour had gone by.

It felt so good, sent little shocks of pleasure into my brain that made my eyes roll back in my head, until I stopped. Then the pain began again, sharp and throbbing.

By that time I was almost totally exposed, my skin thin but almost transparent, useless. It was mostly absent completely everywhere else, bandaged poorly by strips of old clothing I had torn up: I no longer wanted to be in public; no one could see the state I had deteriorated into, so I had no more real bandages. I went back to sleep afterward, letting the blood get all over my bed, drying brown.

I slept peacefully, even then, through the pain, because I was headed toward some sort of resolution. I could feel it. Whether the outcome would be good was anyone's guess.

The first bad omen was when I woke in the morning. My blood had dried to the bedclothes and when I lifted up my arms and legs what flesh was left on them stayed on the bed. It laid there like a hairless cat, veins protruding.

I left my new pet on the sheets; I just put on some sweats, ball cap, and a t-shirt. I was starved: I hadn't eaten anything but an apple here and there (sometimes even rotted ones), maybe a slice of bread, whatever I could find around the apartment. But by that morning I hadn't eaten anything for two days, and my head hurt horribly. I was shaky and exhausted. But I didn't care. I was dying, I knew, so my main plan was to just move forward. It didn't matter where I went, as long as I kept going, like the action was keeping me alive.

I went through my apartment building, cap pulled down over my eyes. The place seemed abandoned. I only passed one person, as they went into their apartment, but I did not meet their gaze. I hoped they didn't see me, bloodied and unkempt, like a leper.

No matter how hard I tried, I just could not make it down the stairs. I had wanted to go down the side stairs, keeping away from any contact I might have with my fellow tenants, but it was too hard. I could only go down two or three steps at a time; I thought maybe I could get down one flight if I was lucky, but seeing how my life was going I should have known I was screwed. After three or four times of panting and holding onto the railing, my legs seconds away from giving out, every step taking all the will I could muster, I finally gave up. I sat down on the bottom step for a while, trying to wake up my legs—they felt asleep, but really weren't—and then I limped out the door onto the third floor. Just move forward. There was one person in the elevator: a very beautiful woman who would not look at me except with fearful eyes.

It was raining, not hard but steady. I didn't put on a jacket, and I could feel every drop of water that fell on my skin, like ice—burning ice. I was shivering uncontrollably by the time I got into the car, and I had only been outside a few moments. I sat, staring blankly, at the steering wheel, hands gripping it tightly, knuckles white but fingers still trembling. It was just like I hit a wall. It was all over. My life, I mean. It was done. There was no way I could continue like this; there was nothing that could make this better. So I sat, empty, letting my mind go nowhere. An hour past before I finally started the engine and began to drive toward the farm.

Once I got out of the town and onto the highway, my spirits lifted. It was like the pulsing of the car and the coming of the horizon ahead drew me forward, like a magnet. Just move forward. I began to go faster and faster. The trees passed my windows as blurs; I wove in and out of the other cars on the highway, almost clipping a few as I cut over. It only took me half the time it should have.

I nearly lost control of the car as I sped down the country back roads. My mind flashed that I wished I had flipped the car, ran it into a tree, but then, just as quickly, I was overjoyed I didn't. For the first time in two months I felt something other than sorrow and pain.

It was a moment of perfect, magical clarity. I had been wasting away for two months, my skin deteriorating, peeling, and bleeding; my mind eroding like rock. I was suddenly so full of life, of hope, of discovery. It was amazing, exhilarating. In that moment, nothing else mattered. Not the farms I passed, not the rumble of my car, not the sweat that had begun to bead on my forehead, not the gnawing pain in my stomach. Nothing mattered but the excitement and the feeling. Then, in the distance: the farmhouse, sitting lonely on the lake.

* * *

It seemed strangely abandoned. There were no animal sounds, no other people. The dog was even gone. There was nothing but the wind.

The yard was overgrown and it looked as if some of the windows were boarded up. As I walked around the back of the farm, I could see the tractor sitting in the middle of the yard, rusted and surrounded by tall weeds. There was a rotting smell in the air—it was definitely strange, out of place, even though I thought for a moment maybe it was coming from me. But it was thick and heavy all around me; it was so strong at one point I gagged. I stood in the clearing, doubled over, trying the catch my breath and then turned around. As I rose up, I saw that the rickety dock was now covering almost half the lake, almost like a makeshift roof over the top that had been abruptly abandoned during its final days of construction. The wood and stones were mossy. I walked closer to the lake; it was nearly half gone, like someone had tried to drain it. There were fish floating on the top, all dead.

I investigated the farm some more. The place was completely desolate. The barn was to my left, the paint faded and cracking off the doors. As I walked closer to the barn, the rotting smell worsened. When I opened the doors, after heaving the latch that held them closed, I was suddenly taken aback. The source of the stink was definitely here.

In a heaped pile were all the animals from the farm—pigs, fowl, even the dog. There were all bloodied, rotted, and crawling with maggots. There was a knife next to the pile, brown with blood. Lying behind the pile, yellowed, dirty, and bruised, was a hand: the farmer's wife. Everyone had been taken into the barn and slaughtered.

Why?

I cautiously stepped forward—why I don't know. It was disgusting, no doubt about it, but I had to look. I guess my curiosity got the best of me. Atop the pile was the dog. I could see that beyond the decomposition of death, its fur was bald in patches, the skin underneath yellowed and crusted, just like my neck had been. Some of the animals were also scarred with blood-filled blisters, just like the ones that had began to grow on my stomach.

Knowing I was on the verge of discovery, I left the barn quickly and started toward the house. The tall grass caught under my pants and dug into my legs like spurs, but I kept on going, walking as fast as I could across the farm. As I approached the house, I saw a light on in the upstairs window, winking through the lace curtains. The door was unlocked, it half-hung open.

Inside it looked remarkably like my apartment. There was inch-thick dust everywhere, cobwebs in the corners, papers and trash strewn about carelessly. The word *decrepit* came into my brain. Everything was wooden, shades of gray and brown, mottled here and there by pale greens and yellows, some white. The little light that managed to get through the dark curtains hung like beacons from heaven onto this deserted place. The air was stale around me. All was still except for a quiet shuffling above me.

An otherworldly pull drew me through the house. There was not much light except from the open door behind me, so I had to walk carefully, but somehow I knew exactly where I was going. The old wallpaper was peeling off the walls, its swirls and crests, its stripes, disjointed and faded. Books were piled high on tables; I nearly knocked over some when I walked straight into a tall end table. I caught the books heavy handedly, sighing with relief when I had put them back safely in their place. I did not want any sounds to give away my presence here: I felt as if I were invading a mausoleum, peeking in on the dead, prying into what was left of their somber existence. The floors were creaky, the boards moaning under my weight, even though I moved slowly, each note seeming to echo.

Suddenly the walls expanded around me: there was a stairwell on my right. There was a window at the top of the stairs, light cutting through the openings of its old, yellow lace curtains. I crept up the stairs slowly, holding onto the banister, one hand over the other, like I was climbing—climbing to my destiny. All this…hell…was leading up to this. There was a light ahead, keeping me moving through my tunnel vision.

I was terrified.

But I just kept moving.

Once I had gotten to the second floor the faint shuffling that had been above me turned into a slow racket. It sounded like someone was moving things around, dragging things across the carpet, pulling things down off the walls. There was a door ahead of me, half open; light poured out from the bare bulb hanging from the ceiling. As I crept closer, I saw it was the old man. I can't remember his name. But he was short and sickly skinny, his hair gray wisps across his forehead. He wore tennis shoes, pajama pants, and a sleeveless undershirt.

All of his skin was bloodied, scaled, blistered, and peeling.

Without thinking, I immediately went into his room. "Went" is too calm a word—I stormed in there, guns blazing. You would think I would have some kind of sympathy for this poor old man, but instead all I had was indescribable anger. He turned when he heard me enter the room, but I was on him before he could do or say anything.

I tackled him to the ground, got on top of him, and punched him in the face, as hard as I could, four, maybe five times. The screaming pains through my ragged hand made me stop—punching. Then I began to kick him, thrusting into his stomach, feeling them plow through the mush of his body. I got on top of him and began to drive my knees into him, wherever I could hit. He gasped and his eyes fluttered to their whites; he coughed, harried breaths that barely came; his lips trembled, a slow trickle of blood coming into the corners and down his cheeks. I picked up his head in both hands and slammed it against the floor. I screamed and cursed and raved.

"You did this to me!" rang in the air as I pulled myself off of him and looked at him in disgust. He began to convulse from the knocks his head had taken. But I had no sympathy. I came here looking for answers, and all I found were more questions. This broken man couldn't fix me; he was broken.

I stepped back and sat on top of an overturned TV stand. I just watched him as he writhed and cried. I knew he was going to die, and I smiled. God help me, I smiled. I delighted in the thought of having killed this man—like if I killed this diseased wretch I would kill the disease in myself.

Was this how low I had gotten?

* * *

Now my anger was gone; a panic had taken its place. I was alone, in this abandoned, disordered house, with a barn full of dead animals, the farmer's wife, and the dead farmer in front of me. This, for certain, was not good.

I left the barn to stink and the body at my feet, and went back downstairs. None of the light switches worked; the sun was beginning to set. I found a box of light bulbs in a kitchen drawer. Once I had replaced some bulbs and turned on some lights, I saw that the house was not actually as trashed as I thought. The kitchen and living room were the only rooms downstairs that had a considerable mess. Upstairs all that was in disarray were the bathroom, pill bottles all over the floor and a musty smell like it had flooded; don't make me explain the state of the bedroom where I had killed the farmer. I can't.

Just like in my apartment, all the mirrors in the house were broken.

On the kitchen table, amid the crushed beer cans, dirty plates, and sticky spills was a stack of papers. They were out of place, crisp and new, white. They had been taken out of a manila envelope which sat just to the left of the stack. It had been carelessly torn open; the top was nearly ripped off. I didn't really look at the return address, but I noticed there was a seal, like a crest. The stack of papers was actually a letter:

7 January 2008

T————W———
Secretary of the Department of——— —
United States Federal Government

Mr. Petrie,

    The U.S. Department of————is conducting a research study on water-born microorganisms. We are asking a select few of our nation's top farmers to participate. You are one of those select candidates. We feel your lake, long known to be the most nutrient-rich in your state, is an ideal location for one of our initial experiments.
    Please fill out and return the enclosed forms for more information.

    T————W————

There was another letter, dated later:

21 January 2008
T————W———
Secretary of the Department of————
United States Federal Government

    Mr. Petrie,

    Thank you for your interest in our new Blue-Green Algae Program. We are very pleased you have decided to participate in our latest study. A representative of our offices will be getting in touch with you shortly to begin your trial.

The type of algae that will be introduced into your lake is a new species of blue-green algae. Our laboratories have developed a new, similar type of algae to possibly help protect our local waters from infestation of its parent, if such an incident should occur. This alga is actually a bacterium, and has been known to become very aggressive. If an attack on our water systems should happen, this new bacteria may be able to "eat" away the problem.

This species, known as cyanobacteria, has been known to produce toxins which are harmful to humans and animals when ingested or through contact with broken skin. Some of the effects of this bacterium, if ingested, can be:

Fatigue
Muscle weakness
Fever
Headache
Large blood blisters
Numbness
Slight yellowing and peeling of the skin

Once the new bacterium has been introduced to your lake, please contact our office immediately if you or your family experiences any of these symptoms.

Thank you,
T———W————

The last letter, on top of the rest of the paperwork; that's all it was—paperwork, carbon papered forms with tiny boxes and lines. It was dated a month later, three days before I read it:

18 February 2008

T———W———
Secretary of the Department of————
United States Federal Government

   Thank you for contacting our offices by phone and mail about your experiment. We would like you to complete the enclosed forms and send them back to us so we can review your situation and determine the correct actions that need to be taken.

   T————W————

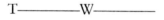

* * *

I couldn't believe it. I had to read the letters twice before I realized what I had read. One of our government's laboratories had made a bacterium that, with the correct exposure, could lead to my disease: the old man's disease, the livestock's disease. They had made this disease as a counter to bio-terrorism and used its own citizens to try it out. When the farmer wrote to them about it, telling them it was killing him, his wife, and his farm, all they did was send him paperwork to fill out. When he saw there was going to be no help, he killed the animals, and his wife, to spare them the pain.

   Did he know that I had the same affliction? Would he have killed me if he knew?

My mind flashed to the bathroom: there were pill bottles strewn across the floor, all of them opened, their contents exposed. Once he had slaughtered everything he had, he tried to kill himself. I had come to the house as he was trying to prepare himself for his death, while he could.

I guess I had finished the job.

But this sickness, how had they gotten it? How did I?

There was a cut on my neck from shaving the morning we went fishing. My feet had gotten wet so I took my shoes off; my hands in turn had gotten wet from the lake water. Then I scratched at the cut. I might have even rubbed it a little.

It was that easy.

I had brought this on myself.

* * *

My name is Andrew Smith. Not a spectacular name, I know, but it is one you should remember. You may not know who I am by name, not now anyway, but you will see my picture on the news soon. You won't see my face: I wear this white, expressionless mask all the time, but you will still see me. I change my wigs from time to time, change my clothing, but somehow I know they'll find me. The government has ways of doing that.

I used to live in the old farmhouse. I filled out the paperwork and sent it back to the ————Department, understating the problem, of course. Saying I was the farmer, I told them was that my fish began to die so I tried to drain the lake. I said that I had gotten scared but still wanted to continue in the experiment, if the worst that would happen was the death of my fish. They assured me that would be the extent of the problem, and that it was actually quite common in the other trials. (If you must know, there were other lakes that became—infected—but everyone involved had been killed "by the disease." Funny how they never mentioned it. You never heard about that on the evening news…but you will soon.)

Anyway, they came back shortly after and refilled the lake. By then the barn was long repaired and the lid on the lake—that's what it was, a lid. The farmer had tried to cover the lake to contain the bacteria; the lid I tore down. You couldn't even tell it had been there. I was, conveniently, *out* when they came back.

And I say *out* because I only come out every few weeks. I travel now, from town to town, living in abandoned buildings, some barns. I take a new dead fish from each of the lakes I go to and drop it in the next lake or water purification plant. It's a continuing cycle, one that I plan to stick with until the assholes that did this to me put me away. Or kill me. I think I would like it if they killed me, because the disease did not.

You see, the disease will eventually stop spreading. Your body, even though it is being attacked by a bacterium that eats it away, will regenerate some flesh once the disease is focused on another area. The human body is amazing like that; it never stops fighting. A person can be riddled with cancer, but it still hangs on. It really does not want to die.

The pain stops eventually as well, and you're just left as one big, bloody mass, your skin falling off, exposing the muscle, muscle giving way to almost show the bone. The disease eats the new tissue that develops but it still regenerates fast enough that you don't die. That is why I wear the mask and the long overcoat.

You do not want to see what is underneath.

But soon enough you will. What you're reading has been sent to all major news channels, complete with security photos of myself as I have committed my acts, to prove this is real. I have written this—confession, you could call it—because I want to give you what I did not have: a warning. I have been to nearly every major city and small town in these United States, infecting the water. The water you drank with dinner last night; the water you brushed your teeth with this morning; the water you showered with; the water you bathed your children in. Almost all of it has the bacteria, and if it doesn't, it soon will. You will get to see what I have become because I have given it to you as well. That athlete's foot: it's probably not that at all. That cut you bandaged for your daughter a few days ago when she fell off her bike? The disease was on your hands, and as you bandaged it, you gave it to her.

This disease will spread and spread. And I will be the cause. I want you to share in my pain, and I want you to know who to thank for that misery.

You've got to gain infamy somehow, right? That's the least you owe me.